W9-AYR-708

CHRISTMAS
IN MY HEART

12

THE CHRISTMAS STORY

And it came to pass in those days, that there went out a decree
from Caesar Augustus, that all the world should be taxed. . . .
And all went to be taxed, every one into his own city. And
Joseph also went up from Galilee, out of the city of Nazareth,
into Judaea, unto the city of David, which is called Bethlehem;
(because he was of the house and lineage of David:) to be taxed
with Mary his espoused wife, being great with child. And so it
was, that, while they were there, the days were accomplished
that she should be delivered. And she brought forth her firstborn
son, and wrapped him in swaddling clothes, and laid him in a
manger; because there was no room for them in the inn.
And there were in the same country shepherds abiding in the field,
keeping watch over their flock by night. And, lo, the angel of
the Lord came upon them, and the glory of the Lord shone
round about them: and they were sore afraid. And the angel said
unto them, Fear not: for, behold, I bring you good tidings of
great joy, which shall be to all people. For unto you is born this
day in the city of David a Saviour, which is Christ the Lord.
And this shall be a sign unto you; Ye shall find the babe wrapped
in swaddling clothes, lying in a manger. And suddenly there was
with the angel a multitude of the heavenly host praising God,
and saying, Glory to God in the highest, and on earth peace,
good will toward men. And it came to pass, as the angels were
gone away from them into heaven, the shepherds said one to
another, Let us now go even unto Bethlehem, and see this thing
which is come to pass, which the Lord hath made known unto
us. And they came with haste, and found Mary, and Joseph, and
the babe lying in a manger. And when they had seen it, they
made known abroad the saying which was told them concerning
this child. . . . And the shepherds returned, glorifying and praising God for all the things that they had heard and seen.

Luke 2:1-20, KJV

FOCUS ON THE FAMILY®

CHRISTMAS IN MY HEART

A TREASURY OF TIMELESS CHRISTMAS STORIES

12

compiled and edited by

JOE L. WHEELER

TYNDALE HOUSE PUBLISHERS, INC., WHEATON, ILLINOIS

14062889

Visit Tyndale's exciting Web site at www.tyndale.com

Visit Joe Wheeler's Web site at www.joewheelerbooks.com

Woodcut illustrations are from the library of Joe L. Wheeler.

Designed by Jenny Swanson.

Published in association with the literary agency of Alive Communications, Inc., 7680 Goddard Street, Suite 200, Colorado Springs, Colorado 80920.

Library of Congress Cataloging-in-Publication Data

Christmas in my heart/ [compiled by] Joe L. Wheeler.
  p. cm.
  ISBN 0-8423-7126-5 (12)
  1. Christmas stories, American. I. Wheeler, Joe L., date

PS648.C45C447   1992

813'.010833—dc20

Printed in Italy

10	09	08	07	06	05	04	03
10	9	8	7	6	5	4	3

DEDICATION

"The Conscience of the World"

These five words sum up the essence of this man's life.

At one time, I knew him merely by reputation, but during the last ten years I have come to know him as a cherished friend. True friends dare to speak truth to each other, even when that truth may hurt. In the crucible of such honesty our friendship has been forged.

Undoubtedly, however, our greatest bond is that we are both moved to tears by those rare stories that touch the heart and soul. Without question, our worldwide ministry of stories would not have come to be without his inspiration, encouragement, and partnership.

For ten years now, I have been closely observing him and his associates, wondering whether or not there might be a crack dividing the talk from the walk. I have not found it. For he is that rarity today: a founder of a great ministry who has remained humble, teachable, and unselfish. A rock of dependability and integrity in an unstable world.

Of course he is not perfect, for none of us are. But his mistakes are sins of *comission* rather than *omission*. A doer *always* makes mistakes, for they are the ladder rungs by which one climbs to success. The important thing is to admit them, profit by them, and build upon them—all of which he has done.

Few leaders are as well-loved as he.

But when all is said, written, and done about this man's life, one role will remain paramount in human memory: He counted it his greatest glory to be an undershepherd to the Great Shepherd, to devotedly and untiringly minister to God's flock.

Thus it gives me great pleasure to dedicate *Christmas in My Heart 12* to

DR. JAMES DOBSON
of
Focus on the Family.

CONTENTS

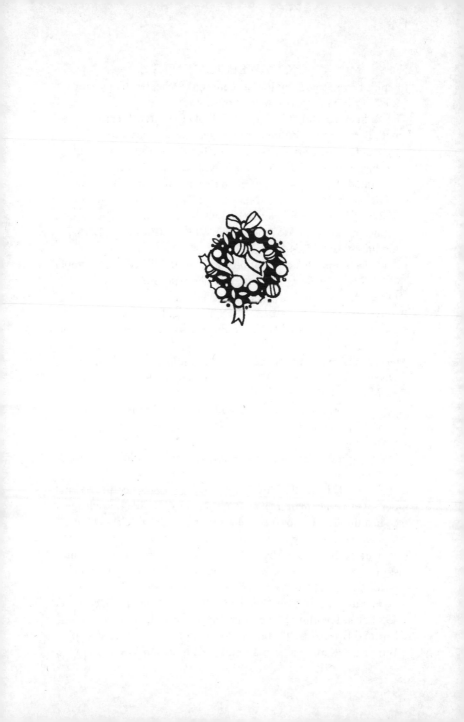

ACKNOWLEDGMENTS

"Joseph's Love Story," by Joseph Leininger Wheeler. Copyright © 2002. Printed by permission of the author.

"The Kidnapped Doll," by Myrtle "Cookie" Potter. Reprinted with permission from *Guideposts* magazine. Copyright © 1993 by Guideposts, Carmel, New York 10512. All rights reserved.

"Van Valkenberg's Christmas Gift," by Elizabeth G. Jordan. Published in Maud Van Buren and Katharine Isabel Bemis's *Christmas in Modern Story* (New York: The Century Company, 1927). If anyone can provide knowledge of earliest publication of this old story, please send to Joe Wheeler (P.O. Box 1246, Conifer, CO 80433).

"Joyful *and* Triumphant," by John McCain. Published in December 1984 *Reader's Digest*. Reprinted by permission of Reader's Digest Association, Inc., and John McCain.

"A Love Song for Christmas," by D. T. Doig. Published in December 1987 *Good Housekeeping*. Reprinted by permission of Rosalind Doig.

"Merry Christmas, Mr. Keene," by Jewell Johnson. Published in December 12 and 19, 2000, issues of *Cappers*. Reprinted by permission of the author.

"A Song Is Born," by Ruth Langland Holberg. Published in *The Girls' Companion*, December 24, 1939. Text reprinted by permission of Joe L. Wheeler (P.O. Box 1246, Conifer, CO 80433) and Cook Communication Ministries, Colorado Springs, Colorado.

"Santa Claus Is Kindness," by Temple Bailey. Published in December 1936 *Good Housekeeping*. If anyone can provide knowledge of first publication source of this old story, please relay to Joe Wheeler (P.O. Box 1246, Conifer, CO 80433).

"Our Part of the Circle," by Joyce Reagin. Reprinted with permission from *Guideposts* magazine. Copyright © 1994 by Guideposts, Carmel, New York 10512. All rights reserved.

"The Family Twinkle," by Nancy N. Rue. Published in December 1993 *Brio*. Reprinted by permission of the author.

"Christmas Bread," by Kathleen Norris. Published in Maud Van Buren and Katharine Isabel Bemis's *Christmas in Modern Story*

(New York: The Century Company, 1927). If anyone can provide knowledge of earliest publication of this old story, please send to Joe Wheeler (P.O. Box 1246, Conifer, CO 80433).

"The Night of the Blizzard," by Lawrence J. Seyler, as told to Sue Philipp. Reprinted with permission from *Guideposts* magazine. Copyright © 1994 by Guideposts, Carmel, New York 10512. All rights reserved.

"The Story of the Field of Angels," by Florence Morse Kingsley. Published in Maud Van Buren and Katharine Isabel Bemis's *Christmas in Storyland* (New York: The Century Company, 1927). If anyone can provide knowledge of earliest publication of this old story, please send to Joe Wheeler (P.O. Box 1246, Conifer, CO 80433).

"The Gift of the Manger," by Edith Barnard Delano. Published in Maud Van Buren and Katharine Isabel Bemis's *Christmas in Modern Story* (New York: The Century Company, 1927). If anyone can provide knowledge of earliest publication of this old story, please send to Joe Wheeler (P.O. Box 1246, Conifer, CO 80433).

"Somewhere I'll Find You," by Donald L. Deffner. Published in December 1996 *The Lutheran Witness*. Reprinted by permission of *The Lutheran Witness*.

"Christmas Sabbatical," by Joseph Leininger Wheeler. Copyright © 2002. Printed by permission of the author.

❄ ❄ ❄

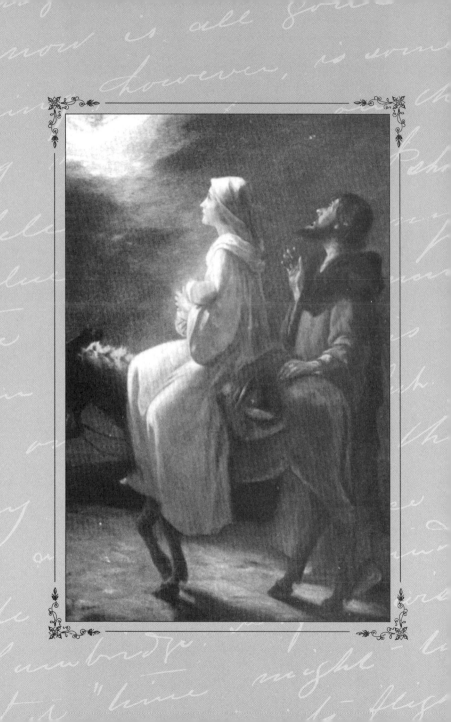

INTRODUCTION: JOSEPH'S LOVE STORY

---

*Strange, isn't it, how we so often miss the obvious—
what was in plain sight all along? How in proofing an
article one may catch every small error in the text yet
miss the most glaring one of all—in the headline, yet!*

*Just so, I submit, it is with the love story of Joseph
and Mary, the human parents of Jesus.*

*"Belaboring the obvious" I might have said only
two weeks ago. But not now. This is the way it
happened: I had been praying for some time that God
would choose the subject for our twelfth* Christmas in
My Heart *introduction. In each one, I attempt to
explore new ground, where Christmas is concerned.*

As time passed, I became convicted that I should write it on the subject of Joseph (our Lord's earthly father). Initially I fought it, as I assumed that I knew most everything there was to know about Joseph already. After doing considerable research and reading and rereading all early scriptural references to Jesus' earthly life, I was forced to admit that my knowledge of Joseph was greatly limited. If that was true of me, I felt it might also be true for many others.

Since neither Mark nor John describes Jesus' life prior to his baptism by John in the Jordan, we will focus on the accounts written by Matthew and Luke. While these accounts give us all we need for theological understanding, they don't satisfy our curiosity in all respects.

PROLOGUE

If this were the typical retelling of the Nativity story, we would leave out the Zechariah-Elizabeth subplot chronicled by Luke. Yet, as we shall see, doing so short-changes our understanding of the complex love story of Joseph and Mary. *With* the Zechariah-Elizabeth story included, note how much more powerful and moving this story becomes!

Thus Luke's story begins not with Mary or Joseph but with the priest Zechariah and his wife, Elizabeth. Both were old ("very old," according to Luke). While Zechariah is ministering in the temple, an angel appears before him, standing at the right of the incense altar. The good priest is terrified, and the angel attempts to put him at ease:

> Don't be afraid, Zechariah! For God has heard
> your prayer, and your wife, Elizabeth, will bear
> you a son! And you are to name him John.
> (Luke 1:13)

Gabriel said much more about how mightily God
would bless the ministry of this son-to-be and how that
son would prepare the way for the coming of the long-
promised Messiah, but poor Zechariah was listening
with only part of his brain. Within the other part,
thoughts like these must have raced about helter-skelter:
*All this sounds wonderful—or at least it would have been
wonderful forty years or so ago when we began awaiting the
child who never came. As the years passed, people began to say
we were cursed—that God was displeased with us. Elizabeth
and I, almost in despair, began to pray daily that God would
heal her barrenness. But God did not. When we grew old, we
ceased praying for a child. My goodness! The mere thought of
having a child at our age is enough to leave me in a cold sweat!
As for Elizabeth, I can just hear her cackle of disbelief were I to
tell her what the angel told me. But I certainly dare not tell all
this to the angel, for I'd seem like an ingrate. Let's see, how
can I respond? Oh, I know!*

> How can I know this will happen? I'm an old man
> now, and my wife is also well along in years. (1:18)

Gabriel was not amused:

> I am Gabriel! I stand in the very presence of God.
> It was he who sent me to bring you this good
> news! And now, since you didn't believe what I

said, you won't be able to speak until the child is born. (1:19-20)

True enough, speech deserted Zechariah from that moment on. Nevertheless, he stayed on at his post until his term of service was over. Apparently, he did his part. About this, Luke is very cryptic:

> Then he returned home. Soon afterward his wife, Elizabeth, became pregnant and went into seclusion for five months. (1:23-24)

With good reason! She must have been in shock, perhaps even suspecting she had a tumor of some sort. But when the truth become inescapable, she reacted much differently than her husband had:

> "How kind the Lord is!" she exclaimed. "He has taken away my disgrace of having no children!" (1:25)

NAZARETH

In the first chapter of his Gospel, Luke introduces us to Mary and Joseph as a sidebar to Elizabeth's pregnancy:

> In the sixth month of Elizabeth's pregnancy, God sent the angel Gabriel to Nazareth, a village in Galilee, to a virgin named Mary. She was engaged to be married to a man named Joseph, a descendant of King David. Gabriel appeared to her and said, "Greetings, favored woman! The Lord is with you!" (1:26-28)

In the Jewish culture of that day, when a boy turned seventeen, he was considered an adult and expected to begin looking for a wife. Maturity came even earlier for girls. When a girl turned thirteen, it was permissible to ask for her hand in marriage. In reality, parents coordinated the process. Once they tested the waters with their son or daughter (mentioning specific local candidates), serious negotiations began. Thus, our story begins some months before Joseph and Mary's betrothal. Joseph's parents had most likely paid a formal call on Mary's parents. Within hours, the entire town was probably aware of the matter, and it was added to the grist of the daily gossip mill. In such a small town, few secrets could be kept for long.

Then came the formal betrothal (or *giddushin*), a key rite of passage in the life of every Jewish man and woman. The *giddushin* was far more than a mere engagement; once it had been negotiated, even though the marriage ceremony had not yet taken place, the couple was considered to be all but married. In fact, the bridegroom-to-be could not end the betrothal except through divorce. So binding was the *giddushin* that if Joseph had died before the marriage ceremony took place, Mary would have been considered his legal widow. In other parts of Palestine, couples were even permitted to have sexual relations with each other during the betrothal. But this was not true in Galilee. There, and in the region to the south, the affianced were expected to remain virgins until the marriage ceremonies and festivities took place.

Since biblical writers sketched out only the broad outlines of the Nativity story, we can fill in the blank spaces solely by educated guessing. The account that follows represents my own attempts at depicting what I think may have happened in the Joseph and Mary story (constructed upon Scriptures).

Not long after Joseph and Mary's betrothal, an angel visited Mary. Brought up in Jewish culture and traditions, she would not have been unduly surprised by the sight of an angel—the surprise was to have an angel addressing her! And she would have been confused. Surely the angel had mistaken her for someone else, someone important.

> Don't be frightened, Mary . . . for God has decided to bless you! You will become pregnant and have a son, and you are to name him Jesus. He will be very great and will be called the Son of the Most High. And the Lord God will give him the throne of his ancestor David. And he will reign over Israel forever; his Kingdom will never end! (1:30-33)

With each word said by Gabriel, Mary's face grew paler. She said to herself, *I just don't understand what these grand-sounding words are all about. Babies don't just happen. It takes two people, and Joseph hasn't even been mentioned!* At this point, she dared to confront Gabriel with the truth, as she perceived it:

> But how can I have a baby? I am a virgin. (1:34)

Gabriel was kinder to her than he was to Zechariah; she was permitted to keep her voice, in spite of her doubts. He replied:

The Holy Spirit will come upon you, and the power of the Most High will overshadow you. So the baby born to you will be holy, and he will be called the Son of God. What's more, your relative Elizabeth has become pregnant in her old age! People used to say she was barren, but she's already in her sixth month. For nothing is impossible with God. (1:35-37)

How could she possibly refute such an argument from a heavenly being? She must have thought, *What can I say? I can't understand all this in the least. It makes my head spin! I suppose it could happen this way, but what will Joseph say? What will my family say? What will the people say? But I don't dare to challenge God's angel. Far better to submit and deal with the results later:*

I am the Lord's servant, and I am willing to accept whatever he wants. May everything you have said come true. (1:38)

Once the heavenly messenger's presence faded from her room, Mary was left alone to ponder the future. The hours that followed must have brought with them almost unbelievable torment. Yes, she accepted and believed Gabriel spoke the truth to her, but what about Joseph? How would he take her becoming pregnant before they "knew" each other in the biblical sense? Would he believe her story? In the cold light of morning, she thought not. This thing would shatter all the dreams they had made for the marriage ceremony, the extended celebration of family and friends, and the honeymoon itself. It was accepted in Jewish society that the newlyweds would be so passionate about each other that they would, in effect, withdraw from society much of the time in order to make love. In fact, the groom could not even be asked to go to war until after a year had passed. Song of Solomon graphically portrays the beauty and intensity of this period.

Mary did not dare go to Joseph with her story. Neither would her parents understand—and there was no doubt at all in her mind that the public would not believe her story. So who would her confidante be? Luke implies that she was finally convinced that the only human being who would understand her predicament was her cousin Elizabeth. Somehow she gained permission from her parents and Joseph to go pay her cousin an extended visit. Quite likely, her parents arranged for the leader of a passing caravan to take her to the hills of Judea, some eighty-five miles away, for it would have been extremely unusual for a teenage girl/woman to make such a trip on her own.

Five days later, Mary arrived at her cousin's house. She entered the house and greeted Elizabeth. At the sound of Mary's greeting, Elizabeth's child leaped within her, and Elizabeth was filled with the Holy Spirit:

> Elizabeth gave a glad cry and exclaimed to Mary, "You are blessed by God above all other women, and your child is blessed. What an honor this is, that the mother of my Lord should visit me! When you came in and greeted me, my baby jumped for joy the instant I heard your voice! [Today we know that the baby in the womb hears everything

said in its vicinity.] You are blessed, because you
believed that the Lord would do what he said."
(1:42–45)

The "Magnificat" that follows is an exquisite hymn of
praise, borrowing heavily from Hannah's song
(1 Samuel 2:1–10). In it, Mary expresses faith, hope,
gratitude, submission, and joy.

Luke tells us that Mary stayed with her cousin three
months, until about the time Elizabeth's baby was born.
Eight days after his birth, at the circumcision ceremony,
pressure was put on the parents to name the baby Zechariah after his father, but Elizabeth declared that he was
to be named John.

> "What?" they exclaimed. "There is no one in all
> your family by that name." So they asked the
> baby's father, communicating to him by making
> gestures. He motioned for a writing tablet, and to
> everyone's surprise he wrote, "His name is John!"
> Instantly Zechariah could speak again, and he
> began praising God. (1:61–64)

Just before John's birth, Mary was able to join a caravan heading back to Nazareth. There was plenty of time
on that long journey home for Mary to ponder all that
she had seen and experienced in recent weeks and
months. She had been stunned by Elizabeth's prophecy
and tribute, for she had mistakenly assumed she was the
only human who knew of the divine baby she would be
carrying in her womb. Make that *was:* She was almost
three months along before she left her cousin.

Now that Mary was returning home, she was forced to deal with harsh realities: How much longer could she keep her secret from her parents, Joseph, and the community? Ruefully she realized that she was already running out of time. Certainly her parents and Joseph would have to know—soon! *Joseph.* She had admired him from afar ever since she'd been a small girl, and until recently she had not even dreamed that the attraction was mutual. Since their betrothal, she had only come to admire, respect, and love him more.

Back home in Nazareth, she waited for Joseph's visit with both longing and dread. How long it was before she told him of all that had taken place, we don't really know. When she finally *did* tell him, it is likely that he either refused to believe her far-fetched explanation for her condition, or he broke into her partially told story with an angry response: "*Nobody* in this town will for a moment believe your story! Neither can I!" and fled from her presence.

During the agonizing hours that followed, Joseph left his boyhood behind him. Day or night, it was all the same: Mary dominated every thought. Once his anger cooled somewhat and he began to consider her story rationally, he began to pity her. Undoubtedly, a man somewhere along the way had taken advantage of Mary's innocence and violated her. Unable to admit the truth to him, she had invented this wildly improbable tale. That she had consented willingly he could not for a moment believe. Even now, her eyes retained the innocence and purity that had been there before her trip to Jerusalem. It was hard to understand.

One thing he did admit to himself during his torment: He loved her still. Most likely, he always would. But having admitted that, he knew he could not go on with this mockery of a betrothal. As he saw it, he had but three options: (1) He could pretend the child was his. He wouldn't do that, for he knew it wasn't. The town would know it all too soon as well. (2) He could shame Mary publicly. He probably shuddered at that thought. Should he do so, Mary would undoubtedly be stoned to death for adultery or cast over a cliff. No, he could not possibly do that to her. (3) He could quietly divorce her and refuse to give reasons. Perhaps he could get her to go away to some other town and start over again. It would be terribly difficult, for both families were poor. There was not even enough money for a dowry. Yes, that third option was the only one he could seriously consider. But oh! To give her up would be like tearing out his heart by the roots! We are not told how long Joseph agonized over this, but we can assume that it may have been for some time.

It is at this point that Matthew picks up the story:

> [Joseph] fell asleep, and an angel of the Lord appeared to him in a dream. "Joseph, son of David," the angel said, "do not be afraid to go ahead with your marriage to Mary. For the child within her has been conceived by the Holy Spirit. And she will have a son, and you are to name him Jesus, for he will save his people from their sins." (Matthew 1:20-21)

When Joseph awoke the next morning, he felt as though he had been reborn during the night: Mary had not lied after all! She was still innocent, she was still pure, she was—miraculously—still a virgin. God picked well when He chose Joseph as the earthly father of His beloved Son. All through his life, Joseph is portrayed as one who never doubted his God. Thus, once the angel had communicated the truth to him, he never doubted again. Instead, he focused all his energies on a solution. There *had* to be a way out! In time, he decided on a plan of action, determining to share it with Mary that very evening.

As for Mary, she had known by Joseph's angry words that it was all over. As day after day passed with no word from him, she could only assume the worst. And short of a miracle, she had no illusions as to what that "worst" would be. When told that he was at the door, she wanted to flee in the other direction.

One look at her haggard, tear-stained face, and Joseph realized that the hell she had endured was worse even than his. He yearned to gather her into his arms and comfort her, but this was no place for it—not with her parents and the neighbors listening to every word. He asked her to go for a walk with him. She now raised her eyes to his, and what she saw there was so unexpected she could only mumble her assent. After a time, they reached a secluded place they both loved. Here, many a time they had reveled in each other's company, planned for their future together, and longed for the day when they would never again have to part. Ever since leaving her house, hope had risen within her. Now she couldn't wait to hear what he had to say.

Even before he had finished telling her of the angelic visitation, joy transfigured her face. So God had not let her down! God had not forgotten her! God had not taken Joseph away from her! The relief was almost more than flesh and blood could handle. More than mere words were needed now, and Joseph was wise enough to see that. In his strong arms she at last found refuge. With his reassurance that he loved and respected her still, and that he would shelter and protect her always, she at last must have just let go: her slight frame shuddering in relief and her tears blending with returning joy.

As for Matthew, how we wish he'd told us more! All he says is this:

> He brought Mary home to be his wife, but she remained a virgin until her son was born. (Matthew 1:24-25)

BETHLEHEM

But taking Mary home to the dwelling Joseph had prepared for her solved only some of her problems. For the people of Nazareth were no different from people today in one respect: they counted backward from a given stage of pregnancy and then they arrived at conclusions. In this case, Mary had only been back from Jerusalem for about five months, yet here she was, almost ready to deliver! Clearly, Joseph was not the biological father. That Joseph forgave her sin and accepted her back, they found nigh unto incredible, especially knowing his legendary sense of justice.

Because he accepted her into his home and extended to her his protection, the townspeople were powerless to injure her physically. Short of that, however, there were a thousand ways they could inflict pain on her. Every time Mary left the house to go to the well for water or to market, she would be subjected to public ridicule, both subtle and overt. She would encounter hissing silence or lacerating words. It got so bad that she dreaded to leave the house—and dreaded even more giving birth to her child in that town. The solution to her problem came from a most unlikely source.

Joseph and Mary lived within the Roman Empire, and the Roman caesars of their time lived so lavishly that they were always in need of money. During Mary's pregnancy, the Roman emperor Augustus decreed that a census be taken. Throughout the empire, all people were required to register in the city of their ancestors. Once they arrived there, each was forced to pay a tax. For both Joseph and Mary, this meant traveling ninety long miles south to Bethlehem, the city of David. Since Mary's condition meant nothing to the imperial tax collectors, staying home was not even an option.

Matthew doesn't explain how or why Jesus came to be born in Bethlehem; he merely declares that He was. Luke fills in a few of the personal details:

> And because Joseph was a descendant of King David, he had to go to Bethlehem in Judea, David's ancient home. He traveled there from the village of Nazareth in Galilee. He took with him Mary, his fiancée, who was obviously pregnant by this time. (Luke 2:4-5)

It was a tough journey—for Joseph, because he walked the entire ninety miles; for Mary, because she rode sidesaddle on their donkey. In her condition, the five days on the road must have seemed much longer. The most beautiful portrayal of the journey I've ever read is found in Jim Bishop's book *The Day Christ Was Born*. In it, Mary and Joseph, once freed from the malevolence exhibited by certain citizens of Nazareth, evidence lighthearted joy. Every step Joseph takes makes Mary respect him more, love him more. He is constantly solicitous of her welfare, and she cannot help comparing her situation to what could have been had Joseph rejected the angel's story.

Strength, wisdom, and tenderness: three qualities women have admired since the world first began. And Joseph embodied all three.

In Bethlehem, it was Joseph who tirelessly sought lodging for Mary, whose time of delivery was only hours away. He found the manger for her and was with her during the agony of childbirth. He was there to receive both the uncouth shepherds and later the regal magi, treating each with courtesy and respect. He was there in the temple for the circumcision on the baby's eighth day. He was there when the aged Simeon (who had been promised that he would not die until he had seen the Messiah) took the baby in his arms and declared that he could now die in peace. He was there when the elderly prophetess Anna declared that this baby was the long-promised King.

The angels spoke no more to Mary, but three times more an angel spoke directly to Joseph. First, the angel directed him to take Mary and the baby and flee to Egypt. King Herod planned to kill the child to prevent Him from usurping the throne. So Joseph fled with his family and bore the brunt of the long, arduous trek through the desert all the way to Egypt. Once in Egypt, Joseph found work among the million or so Hebrew expatriates. The holy family remained there until after Herod's death. An angel came to Joseph a second time to inform him that Herod was now dead, so he could take his family back to Palestine. The third message came in a dream when Joseph was warned to change his travel plans by taking his family on a long, circuitous route around the domain of Herod's son Archelaus.

Each step of the way, Joseph was there: there for Jesus' first wobbly step, for His first spoken word. Later on, Jesus frequently strayed away from His mother so that He could watch His father at work in the carpenter shop. Initially, Joseph was always stumbling over Him, but in time the boy became ever more useful as an assistant, eventually as a partner. It was in this carpenter shop that Jesus asked many of the most important questions a child can ask. Joseph took each one seriously, as did Mary. Perhaps it was partly due to this parental teamwork that Jesus was able to astonish the greatest Jewish thought-leaders of the age with His wisdom and crystal-clear thinking when only twelve years old.

Over time, in this brutally hard wood-hewing occupation (no power tools then!), Christ gradually developed great physical strength and a physique that was strong enough to carry Him through the arduous years of crisscrossing Palestine on foot.

Joseph was there also to lead in all the sacred holiday traditions. He zealously kept them all and transmitted their significance to the boy Jesus. When Jesus was "lost" in the temple for three days, Joseph and Mary finally found Him and took Him home.

When Jesus became a teenager and entered more deeply into the man's world of Judaism, Joseph led the way.

And each day, Jesus saw His father's continuous solicitude and tender love for Mary. The strongest proof of this is our Lord's tender treatment of His mother after He came of age.

Sadly, Joseph apparently did not live to see his son's great ministry. He just drops out of the picture. Had Joseph still been alive at the time of the Cross, Jesus would never have asked His disciple John to be a surrogate son to Mary. As for Jesus' own blood brothers, we know that they did not initially believe in Jesus' divinity—but some came to believe in Him later. Many biblical scholars believe that Joseph's untimely death forced Jesus to become head of the family, working hard as a carpenter until His brothers grew old enough to go out on their own—and that this was the reason He did not begin His public ministry until He was thirty.

Even during Christ's ministry, the long shadow of Joseph's life could often be felt. So faithful had he been that speculation about the parentage of Jesus rarely surfaced anymore:

> He's just a carpenter's son, and we know Mary, his mother, and his brothers—James, Joseph, Simon, and Judas. All his sisters live right here among us. What makes him so great? (Matthew 13:55-56)

> They said, "This is Jesus, the son of Joseph. We
> know his father and mother. How can he say, 'I
> came down from heaven'?" (John 6:42)

The role of Mary in our Savior's earthly life has been eulogized so continually that there is little need for me to expand upon it. Joseph, however, is another story. All too often we treat him merely as a Nativity stage prop, ignoring the fact that God communicated with him through the words of angels three times more than He did with Mary. It is *Joseph's* Davidic lineage that Scripture refers to so often in connection with Jesus Christ. And we shall not know until the new earth if Jesus' DNA included strains from Joseph's line as well as Mary's. It is certainly a distinct possibility in this wondrous intertwining of the human and the divine that was Christ incarnate.

If one word could be used to define Joseph's life, it would be *faithful.* At every step of the way, he was there. He was the rock upon which Mary's adult life was built and upon which most of Jesus' life was built. It is passing strange, is it not, that his role in "The Greatest Story Ever Told" has been so downplayed during the last twenty centuries—even today.

On this subject, note Pulitzer and Nobel prize–winning author Pearl Buck's poignant observations:

> Today, as I think of holly wreaths and gifts, I
> ponder again, as I have so often before, the scene
> of Mary and Joseph and the Child. There is pathos
> in that scene. . . . Generations of painters have
> painted the Holy Family, and their emotions and

hidden feelings about Man, Woman and Child, the Holy Three, have flowed from the brushes they put upon canvas. The woman is the center and she it is who holds the Child. She has always the same face—calm, fulfilled, at peace. She has achieved the purpose for which she was created. . . . And why is the man Joseph always in the shadows? He is a patient, weary man, leaning upon a staff. He has a sober, dutiful air. He seems dubious of his part in the creation. . . . It seems to me, even at this distance, that while he loves the Woman and the Child, he is not quite sure of his place with them. She looks so confident of herself, so sweetly proud of what she has produced. He wonders forever, perhaps, what he has to do with the other two, to whom nevertheless he is inescapably attached and for whose welfare he feels it is his duty to work. I have seen many such patient Josephs, standing in the shadows behind the Woman and the Child. There is a patient Joseph hidden perhaps in every man, and I wonder if it is against this hidden Joseph in himself that every man at some time in his life rebels? . . .

O Joseph, man, come out of the shadow of your fears and stand beside the two you love! (Buck, 107, 108, 123)

As Buck points out, it is indeed long overdue for Christendom to restore Joseph to his rightful place in the Nativity story, but more than that, to his rightful place as the devoted sweetheart, husband, and partner of Mary, as well as the father, teacher, and mentor of Jesus.

He should be included, not in a cameo role, but as one of the three protagonists.

Joseph is among the most faithful and loving men who ever lived!

SOURCES
In addition to the Bible, these are the sources I found most helpful in this research:

Bishop, Jim. *The Day Christ Was Born*. New York: Harper & Brothers, 1960.

Buck, Pearl. "Thoughts of a Woman at Christmas." In *Once Upon a Christmas*. New York: The John Day Company, 1973.

Miller, Madeleine S., and J. Lane Miller. *Harper's Bible Dictionary*. New York: Harper & Brothers, 1952, 1954.

Ward, Kaari, ed. *Jesus and His Times*. Pleasantville, N.Y.: Reader's Digest Association, 1987.

Yancey, Philip. *The Jesus I Never Knew*. Grand Rapids, Mich.: Zondervan Publishing House, 1995.

Encyclopedia Britannica, 1946 ed., vols. 13, 14.

ABOUT THIS TWELFTH COLLECTION
In this second Christmas anthology of our second decade, we continue to introduce authors new to the series. Some are fairly contemporary, such as Myrtle "Cookie" Potter, John McCain, Joyce Reagin, Sue Philipp, Jewell Johnson, and Donald Deffner. Others, such as Elizabeth G. Jordan, Ruth Langland Holberg, Kathleen Norris, Florence Morse Kingsley, and Edith Barnard Delano, were once well known—if not nationally famous—but are, sadly, little known today. What a joy to help bring them back!

And some, such as David T. Doig, Temple Bailey, and Nancy Rue, are already beloved by our readers because of stories anthologized in our earlier books.

But what makes this collection unique and extraspecial is that it is the first of our anthologies to center on the Nativity story. The lead Scripture and the introduction focus on the theme; tying into the Nativity also are "Joyful *and* Triumphant," "Merry Christmas, Mr. Keene," "A Song Is Born," "Santa Claus Is Kindness," "The Night of the Blizzard," "The Story of the Field of Angels," "The Gift of the Manger," and "Somewhere I'll Find You."

May you be blessed!

CODA

I look forward to hearing from you! Please do keep the stories, responses, and suggestions coming—and not just for Christmas stories. I am putting together collections centered around other genres as well. You may reach me by writing to:

Joe L. Wheeler, Ph.D.
c/o Tyndale House Publishers
351 Executive Drive
Carol Stream, IL 60188

May the Lord bless and guide the ministry of these stories in your home.

THE KIDNAPPED DOLL

Oh, how she longed for that doll! She decided to peek under the Christmas tree and see if it was there. It was, but it was for another little girl.

Then came the great temptation.

*I*t was Christmas Eve and the family was gathered at my grandparents' house in San Francisco. I was six that year and my cousin Tom, eight.

We'd waited for months, and now that the time for gift-giving was almost near, every moment seemed a lifetime. Would I get the baby doll I longed for—the one in the window of Mrs. O'Connor's variety store? For months I'd spent part of every day staring at her with my nose pressed against the pane. I was certain that baby doll looked sad every time I left.

"Why don't they give out the presents right now?" I asked. "Why do we have to wait until after dinner?"

"I *can't* wait," said Tom. "Let's sneak into the living room. Maybe we can find out what we're getting."

"Grandpa and the uncles are out in the garden," I said. And our cousins Dorothy, Mildred and Mabel were in the attic playing dress-up.

We peeked in the kitchen. The aroma of fresh-baked bread and roasting turkey with sage dressing filled the air. Grandma smiled as she chopped onions. Aunt Agnes and Aunt Susan bumped happily against each other as they stirred the gravy. But Aunt Margaret scowled as she basted the turkey. "You can't come in here," she said, shaking her spoon at us.

So far so good. Everyone was accounted for. We hurried down the hall to the front of the house and cautiously turned the knob on the living-room door. My heart beat fast. This was forbidden territory until after dinner. We both took a deep breath and Tom pushed the door open.

What a sight! The magnificent pine tree, aglow with lights of every color, was covered with tinsel and bright ornaments. On the top an angel rested serenely, his sparkling wings brushing the ceiling.

"Wow," whispered Tom. "Look at the presents." The rug was covered with gifts. He fell to the floor and started to shake the boxes that bore his name. "This one's just clothes, I think, but doesn't this one sound like an Erector set?"

I was too busy to answer. One of my packages smelled like perfume, another like chocolate. But where was a box that might hold a baby doll? I glanced around the room and spied something covered with a quilt behind a couch. I rushed to it and lifted the cover. Underneath was a buggy— with a doll inside. "My baby!" I cried, picking her up and hugging her.

"Put her back," hissed Tom, yanking my arm. "That doll's not yours. See, the tag says 'To Dorothy.'"

I refused to look. "She's *mine*," I insisted, jerking away. "I've wanted her forever. Santa just made a mistake putting Dorothy's name on her."

Clutching the doll, I ran down the hall and out the back door to Grandpa's workshop. Quickly I thrust the baby onto a pile of wood shavings behind a stack of lumber.

Tom came storming in after me. "You're a kidnapper and a thief," he cried. Then, losing interest, he announced he was going inside. I ran behind him. Tom's last remark worried me: "Do you think you're the only one who wanted a doll? Dorothy asked Santa for a baby too."

I hadn't thought of that. What if it really *was* hers? Her parents would be upset that the doll was missing. Tom would tell on me. Mama would be ashamed. Aunt Margaret would stare down her nose at me, just like her stuck-up daughter, Dorothy.

If that doll was Dorothy's I'd never hear the end of it. Why had I taken her? I had to put her back. My heart beating wildly, I ran as fast as I could to Grandpa's workshop and was about to open the door when I heard voices. Grandpa was in there showing Uncle Edward the cabinet he was building. I couldn't go in now.

Just then Grandma called us to dinner. Shakily I climbed the steps to the house.

In the dining room we bowed our heads as Grandpa said grace. "We thank you, Lord," he began, "for letting us all be together on the day of Jesus' birth." I almost choked. It was bad enough to be a thief and a kidnapper, but to think I'd done it all on baby Jesus' birthday!

After that I had no appetite. When our mothers finally cleared the table and started to do the dishes, I hurried back to the workshop, hoping I could get the doll. But Grandpa was in there again, this time with Uncle Archie.

When we finally gathered in the living room, my face felt hot. The party dress Mama had made me seemed too tight around my neck.

Grandpa began calling names and giving out presents. He waited for each person to open the gift before he called another name. I stole a look at Tom; he was totally involved in unwrapping his own packages. After an hour, Dorothy's buggy was still behind the couch. Though I'd received several presents, Mama could see I wasn't happy. She left the room and came back wheeling a doll buggy. "Santa left this for Myrtle," she said.

I gasped. Inside was a doll better than the one I'd taken. She had a different dress, a pretty bonnet and a coverlet of pink and blue satin. She wore a ruffled petticoat, lace panties and bootees. I knew Mama had made them; the blanket was of the same satin she'd used to make Grandma a robe. My baby was so special that I hugged her right then and vowed never to let her go.

Suddenly I felt sick to my stomach. For a moment I'd forgotten Dorothy's doll. It was still missing.

"What's the matter, Myrtle?" said Mama. "Don't you like her?"

"Oh, Mama, I *love* her."

But of course I couldn't enjoy my present until I put Dorothy's doll back. How could I possibly do it? Jesus! It was His birthday. Maybe He could help me. *Jesus, I prayed silently, I'm sorry I was so bad. Please help me make things right.*

Grandpa called for attention. "We've got a lot more presents to give out. But we're going to take a recess. Pumpkin pie with whipped cream is waiting in the dining room."

This was my chance! As everyone headed for dessert, I stole out the back door and down the steps. This time no one was in the workshop. Behind the lumber, with her dress askew and wood shavings in her hair, lay Dorothy's doll. I grabbed her and got her back to the living room without being seen. I picked the shavings out of her hair, smoothed her clothes, and started to put her in the buggy behind the couch.

But my heart sank when I saw a pink smear on her cheek. Grandpa painted landscapes and there must have been a drop of paint on the wood shavings. Rub as I might, I couldn't get it off. Dorothy and Aunt Margaret would be sure to notice it.

I knew what I had to do. With trembling fingers I undressed both dolls. I put Dorothy's doll clothes on my perfect doll, and the clothes Mama had made on the doll with the smudged cheek. I put the perfect doll in Dorothy's buggy and the one I'd kidnapped in my buggy, with her smeared cheek against the pillow.

When everyone returned to the living room, Grandpa finished giving out the presents. Dorothy received her doll and was just as happy with her as I had been with mine.

"Our dolls look like twins," I said. "Let's have a tea party for them."

"That'll be fun," said Dorothy. "I'll bring cookies."

She's not stuck-up, I told myself. *I'm sure we can be friends.*

"Mama," I said that night as I was getting into bed, "I'm naming my doll Mary, after Jesus' mother."

"That's lovely," said Mama. "You know, your doll has a little pink mark on her cheek. Mrs. O'Connor has a lot of other dolls in her store. I'm sure we can exchange her."

"No," I cried. "I like her just the way she is."

I snuggled in my blanket, holding Mary close, filled with an overwhelming joy that had nothing to do with dolls or buggies. I was only six years old but already I'd sensed it: When you do something bad, it's possible, with God's help, to make things right.

Myrtle "Cookie" Potter
Myrtle "Cookie" Potter of San Mateo, California, writes for contemporary family and inspirational magazines.

Elizabeth G. Jordan

VAN VALKENBERG'S
CHRISTMAS GIFT

---

*It was many years ago that I first read this Christmas
story. Then it turned truant and wandered away. In
time, I forgot about it. But, just days before I
finalized our twelfth collection, here it came, a bit
sheepish about its long absence. Nevertheless, it gazed
trustingly at me, daring me to reject it.*

*How could I? I opened my arms and welcomed the
beloved prodigal home. Its time had come.*

*T*he "Chicago Limited" was pulling out of the Grand Central Station in New York as Dr. Henry Van Valkenberg submitted his ticket to the gateman. He dashed through, pushing the indignant official to one side, and made a leap for the railing of the last car of the train. It was wet and slippery and maddeningly elusive, but he caught it, and clung to it valiantly, his legs actively seeking a resting-place on the snow-covered steps of the platform. Even as he hung there, offering to his fellow-travelers this inspiring illustration of athletic prowess and the strenuous life, he was painfully conscious that the position was not a dignified one for a stout gentleman of sixty with an exalted position in the scientific world. He pictured to himself the happy smiles of those who were looking on, and he realized that his conception of their hearty enjoyment had not been exaggerated when he glanced back at them after a friendly brakeman had dragged him "on board." Dr. Van Valkenberg smiled a little ruefully as he thanked the man and rubbed the aching surface of his hand, which not even his thick kid gloves had protected. Then he pulled himself together, picked up the books and newspapers he had dropped and which the bystanders had enthusiastically hurled after him, and sought his haven in the sleeping-car. When he reached his section he stood for a moment, with his back to the passengers, to put some of his belongings in the rack above his head. As he was trying to arrange them properly he heard a voice behind him.

"O-oh! Were you hurt?" it said. "I was so 'fraid you were going to fall."

Dr. Van Valkenberg, who was a tall man, turned and

looked down from his great height. At his feet stood a baby; at least she seemed a baby to him, although she was very dignified and wholly self-possessed and fully four years old. She was looking up at him with dark brown eyes, which wore an absurdly anxious expression. In that instant of quick observation he noticed that her wraps had been removed and that she wore a white dress and had yellow curls, among which, on one side of her head, a small black bow lay sombrely.

She was so delightful in her almost maternal solicitude that he smiled irrepressibly, though he answered with the ceremoniousness she seemed to expect.

"Why, no, thank you," he said. "I am not hurt. Didn't you see the kind man help me onto the car?"

There was a subdivided titter from the other passengers over this touching admission of helplessness, but the human atom below drew a long, audible sigh of relief.

"I'm very glad," she said, with dignity. "I was 'fraid he hurt you." She turned as she spoke, and toddled into the section opposite his, where a plain but kindly faced elderly woman was sitting. She lifted her charge to the seat beside her, and the child rose to her knees, pressed her pink face against the window-pane, and looked out at the snow that was falling heavily.

Dr. Van Valkenberg settled back in his seat and tried to read his newspaper, but for some reason the slight incident in which he and the little girl had figured moved him strangely. It had been a long time since anyone had looked at him like that! He was not a person who aroused sympathy. He conscientiously endeavored to follow the President's latest oracular utterances on the Trust problem, but his eyes turned often to the curly head at the window opposite. They were well-trained, observant eyes, and they read the woman as not the mother, but a paid attendant—a trained nurse, probably, with fifteen years of admirable, cold, scientific service behind her. Why was she with the child, he wondered.

It was Christmas eve—not the time for a baby girl to be traveling. Then his glance fell again on the black bow among the yellow curls and on the white dress with its black shoulder-knots,[1] and the explanation came to him. An orphan, of course, on her way West to a new home, in the charge of the matter-of-fact nurse who was dozing comfortably in the corner of her seat. To whom was she going? Perhaps to grandparents, where she would be spoiled and wholly happy; or quite possibly to more distant relatives where she might find a grudging welcome. Dear little embryo woman, with her sympathetic heart already attuned to the world's gamut of pain. She should have been dancing under a Christmas tree, or hanging up her tiny stocking in the warm chimney-corner of some cozy nursery. The heart of the man swelled at the thought, and he recognized the sensation with a feeling of surprised annoyance. What was all this to him—to an old bachelor who knew nothing of children except their infantile ailments, and who had supposed that he cared for them as little as he understood them? Still, it was Christmas. His mind swung back to that. He himself had rebelled at the unwelcome prospect of Christmas eve and Christmas day in a sleeping-car—he, without even nephews and nieces to

[1]In earlier times, surviving family wore black for an extended period after the death of a close family member.

lighten the gloom of his lonely house. The warm
human sympathy of the man and the sweet traditions of
his youth rose in protest against the spectacle of a lonely
child, traveling through the night toward some distant
home which she had never seen, and where coldness,
even neglect, might await her. Then he reminded
himself that this was all imagination, and that he might
be wholly wrong in his theory of the journey, and he
called himself a fool for his pains. Still, the teasing interest and an elusive but equally teasing memory held his
thoughts.

Darkness was falling, but the porter had not begun to
light the lamps, and heavy shadows were rising from the
corners of the car. Dr. Van Valkenberg's little neighbor
turned from the gloom without to the gloom within,
and made an impulsive movement toward the drowsy
woman opposite her. The nurse did not stir, and the
little girl sat silent, her brown eyes shining in the half-
light and her dimpled hands folded in her lap. The
physician leaned across the aisle.

"Won't you come over and visit me?" he asked. "I
am very lonely, and I have no one to take care of me."

She slid off the seat at once, with great alacrity.

"I'd like to," she said, "but I must ask Nana. I must
always ask Nana now," she added, with dutiful empha-
sis, "'fore I do anything."

She laid her hand on the gloved fingers of the nurse
as she spoke, and the woman opened her eyes, shot a
quick glance at the man, and nodded. She had not been
asleep. Dr. Van Valkenberg rose and lifted his visitor to
the seat beside him, where her short legs stuck out in
uncompromising rigidity, and her tiny hands returned

demurely to their former position in her lap. She took up the conversation where it had been interrupted.

"I can take care of you," she said, brightly. "I taked care of mamma a great deal, and I gave her her med'cin'."

He replied by placing a cushion behind her back and forming a resting-place for her feet by building an imposing pyramid, of which his dressing-case was the base. Then he turned to her with a smile.

"Very well," he said. "If you really are going to take care of me I must know your name. You see," he explained, "I might need you to get me a glass of water or something. Just think how disappointing it would be if I should call you by the wrong name and some other little girl came!"

She laughed.

"You say funny things," she said, contentedly. "But there isn't any other little girl in the car. I looked, soon as I came on, 'cos I wanted one to play with. I like little girls. I like little boys, too," she added, with innocent expansiveness.

"Then we'll play I'm a little boy. You'd never believe it, but I used to be. You haven't told me your name," he reminded her.

"Hope," she said, promptly. "Do you think it is a nice name?" She made the inquiry with an anxious interest which seemed to promise immediate change if the name displeased him. He reassured her.

"I think Hope is the nicest name a little girl could have, except one," he said. "The nicest little girl I ever knew was named Katharine. She grew to be a nice big girl, too, and has little girls of her own now, no doubt," he added, half to himself.

"Were you a little boy when she was a little girl?" asked his visitor, with flattering interest.

"Oh, no; I was a big man, just as I am now. Her father was my friend, and she lived in a white house with an old garden where there were all kinds of flowers. She used to play there when she was a tiny baby, just big enough to crawl along the paths. Later she learned to walk there, and then the gardener had to follow her to see that she didn't pick *all* the flowers. I used to carry her around and hold her high up so she could pull the apples and pears off the trees. When she grew larger I gave her a horse and taught her to ride. She seemed like my very own little girl. But by-and-by she grew up and became a young lady, and—well, she went away from me, and I never had another little girl."

He had begun the story to interest the child. He found, as he went on, that it still interested him.

"Did she go to heaven?" asked the little girl, softly.

"Oh, dear, no," answered the doctor, with brisk cheerfulness.

"Then why didn't she keep on being your little girl always?" was the next leading question.

The doctor hesitated a moment. He was making the discovery that after many years old wounds can reopen and throb. No one had ever been brave enough to broach to him the subject of this single love-affair, which he was now discussing, he told himself, like a garrulous old woman. He was anxious to direct the conversation into other channels, but there was a certain compelling demand in the brown eyes upturned to his.

"Well, you see," he explained, "other boys liked her, too. And when she became a young lady other men liked her. So finally—one of them took her away from me."

He uttered the last words wearily, and the sensitive atom at his side seemed to understand why. Her little hand slipped into his.

"Why didn't you ask her to please stay with you?" she persisted, pityingly.

"I did," he told her. "But, you see, she liked the other man better."

"Oh-h-h." The word came out long-drawn and breathless. "I don't see how she possedly could!"

There was such sorrow for the victim and scorn for the offender in the tone, that, combined with the none too subtle compliment, it was too much for Dr. Van Valkenberg's self-control. He threw back his gray head, and burst into an almost boyish shout of laughter, which effectually cleaned the atmosphere of sentimental memories. He suddenly realized, too, that he had not been giving the child the cheerful holiday evening he had intended.

"Where are you going to hang up your stockings tonight?" he asked. A shade fell over her sensitive face.

"I can't hang them up," she answered, soberly. "Santa Claus doesn't travel on trains, Nana says. But p'r'aps he'll have something waiting for me when I get to Cousin Gertie's," she added, with sweet hopefulness.

"Nana is always right," said the doctor solemnly, "and of course you must do exactly as she says. But I heard that Santa Claus was going to get on the train tonight at Buffalo, and I believe," he added, slowly and impressively, "that if he found a pair of small black stockings hanging from that section he'd fill them!"

Her eyes sparkled.

"Then I'll ask Nana," she said. "An' if she says I may hang them, I will. But one," she added, conscientiously, "has a teeny, weeny hole in the toe. Do you think he would mind that?"

He reassured her on this point, and turned to the nurse, who was now wide awake and absorbed in a novel. The car was brilliantly lighted, and the passengers were beginning to respond to the first dinner call.

"I beg your pardon," he said. "I've taken a great fancy to your little charge, and I want your help to carry out a plan of mine. I have suggested to Hope that she hang up her stockings tonight. I have every reason to believe that Santa Claus will get on this train at Buffalo. In fact," he added, smiling, "I mean to telegraph him."

The nurse hesitated a moment. He drew his cardcase from his pocket and handed her one of the bits of pasteboard it contained.

"I have no evil designs," he added, cheerfully. "If you are a New-Yorker you may possibly know who I am."

The woman's face lit up as she read the name. She turned toward him impulsively, with a very pleasant smile.

"Indeed I do, doctor," she said. "Who does not? Dr. Abbey sent for you last week," she added, "for a consultation over the last case I had—this child's mother. But you were out of town. We were all so disappointed. It seems strange that we should meet now."

"Patient died?" asked the physician, with professional brevity.

"Yes, doctor."

He rose from his seat.

"Now that you have my credentials," he added, cordially, "I want you and Hope to dine with me. You will, won't you?"

The upholstered cheerfulness of the dining-car found favor in the sight of Hope. She conducted herself, however, with her usual dignity, broken only occasionally by an ecstatic wriggle as the prospective visit of Santa Claus crossed her mind. Her dinner, superintended by an eminent physician and a trained nurse, was naturally a simple and severely hygienic one, but here, too, her admirable training was evident. She ate cheerfully her bowl of bread and milk, and wasted no longing glances on the plum-pudding.

Later, in the feverish excitement of hanging up her stockings, going to bed, and peeping through the curtains to catch Santa Claus, a little of her extraordinary repose of manner deserted her; but she fell asleep at last, with great reluctance.

When the curtains round her berth had ceased trembling, a most unusual procession wended its silent way toward Dr. Van Valkenberg's section. In some secret manner the news had gone from one end to the other of the "Special" that a little girl in section nine, car *Floradora,* had hung up her stockings for Santa Claus. The hearts of fathers, mothers, and doting uncles responded at once. Suitcases were unlocked, great trunks were opened, mysterious bundles were unwrapped, and from all these sources came gifts of surprising fitness. Small daughters and nieces, sleeping in Western cities, might well have turned restlessly in their beds had they seen the presents designed for them drop into a pair of tiny stockings and pile up on the floor below.

❋ ❋ ❋

A succession of long-drawn, ecstatic breaths and happy gurgles awoke the passengers on car *Floradora* at an unseemly hour Christmas morning, and a small white figure, clad informally in a single garment, danced up and down the aisle, dragging carts and woolly lambs behind it. Occasionally there was the squeak of a talking doll, and always there was the patter of small feet and the soft cooing of a child's voice, punctuated by the exquisite music of a child's laughter. Dawn was just approaching, and the lamps, still burning, flared pale in the gray light. But in the length of that car there was no soul so base as to long for silence and the pillow. Crabbed old faces looked out between the curtains and smiled; eyes long unused to tears felt a sudden, strange moisture.

Dr. Van Valkenberg had risen almost as early as Hope, and possibly the immaculate freshness of his attire, contrasted with the scantiness of her own, induced that young lady to retire from observation for a short time and emerge clothed for general society. Even during this brief retreat in the dressing-room the passengers heard her breathless voice, high-pitched in her excitement, chattering incessantly to the responsive Nana.

Throughout the day the snow still fell, and the outside world seemed far away and dreamlike to Dr.

Van Valkenberg. The real things were this train, cutting its way through the snow, and this little child, growing deeper into his heart with each moment that passed. The situation was unique, but easy enough to understand, he told himself. He had merely gone back twenty-five years to that other child whom he had cherished. He had been very lonely—how lonely he had only recently begun to realize, and he was becoming an old man whose life lay behind him. He crossed the aisle suddenly and sat down beside the nurse, leaving Hope singing her doll to sleep in his section. There was something almost diffident in his manner as he spoke.

"Will you tell me all you know about the child?" he asked. "She interests me greatly, probably because she's so much like someone I used to know."

The nurse closed her book and looked at him curiously. She had heard much of him, but nothing that would explain this interest in a strange child. He himself could not have explained it. He knew only that he felt it, powerfully and compellingly.

"Her name is Hope Armitage," she said, quietly. "Her mother, who has just died, was a widow—Mrs. Katharine Armitage. They were poor, and Mrs. Armitage seemed to have no relations. She had saved a little, enough to pay most of her expenses at the hospital, and—" She hesitated a moment, and then went on: "I am telling you everything very frankly, because you are you, but it was done quietly enough. We all loved the woman. She was very unusual, and patient, and charming. All the nurses who had had anything to do with her cried when she died. We felt that she might have been saved if she had come to us in time, but she was worked out. She had earned her living by sewing, after her husband's death, three years ago, and she kept at it day and night. She hadn't much constitution to begin with, and none when she came to us. She was so sweet, so brave, yet so desperately miserable over leaving her little girl alone in the world—"

Dr. Van Valkenberg sat silent. It was true, then. This was Katharine's child. Had he not known it? Could he have failed to know it, whenever or wherever they had met? He had not known of the death of Armitage nor of the subsequent poverty of his widow, but he had known Katharine's baby, he now told himself, the moment he saw her.

"Well," the nurse resumed, "after she died we raised a small fund to buy some clothes for Hope, and take her to Chicago to her new home. Mrs. Armitage has a cousin there, who has agreed to take her in. None of the relatives came to the funeral; there are not many of them, and the Chicago people haven't much money, I fancy. They offered to send Hope's fare, or even to come for her if it was absolutely necessary; but they seemed very much relieved when we wrote that I would bring her out."

Dr. Van Valkenberg did not speak at once. He was hardly surprised. Life was full of extraordinary situations, and his profession had brought him face to face with many of them. Nevertheless, a deep solemnity filled him and a strange peace settled over him. He turned to the nurse with something of this in his face and voice.

"I want to take care of her," he said, briefly. "Her mother and father were old friends of mine, and this thing looks like fate. Will they give her to me—these Chicago people—do you think?"

Tears filled the woman's eyes.

"Indeed they will," she said, "and gladly. There was"—she hesitated—"there was even some talk of sending her to an institution before they finally decided to take her. Dear little Hope—how happy she will be with you!"

He left her, and went back to the seat where Hope sat, crooning to the doll. Sitting down, he gathered them both up in his arms, and he smiled as he looked at Hope's yellow curls. Katharine's child—her little helpless baby—now his child, to love and care for. He was not a religious man; nevertheless a prayer rose spontaneously in his heart. But there was a plea to be made—a second plea, somewhat like the one he had made the mother; this time he felt that he knew the answer.

"Hope," he said, gently, "once, long ago, I asked a little girl to come and live with me, and she would not come. Now I want to ask you to come, and stay with me always, and be my own little girl, and let me take care of you and make you happy. Will you come?"

The radiance of June sunshine broke out upon her face and shone in the brown eyes upturned to his. How well he knew that look! Hope did not turn toward Nana, and that significant omission touched him deeply. She seemed to feel that here was a question she alone must decide. She drew a long breath as she looked up at him.

"Really, truly?" she asked. Then, as he nodded without speaking, she saw something in his face that was new to her. It was nothing to frighten a little girl, for it was very sweet and tender; but for one second she thought her new friend was going to cry! She put both arms around his neck, and replied softly, with the exquisite maternal cadences her voice had taken on in her first words to him when he entered the car: "I'll be your own little girl, and I'll take care of you, too. You know, you said I could."

Dr. Van Valkenberg turned to the nurse.

"I shall go with you to her cousin's, from the train," he announced. "I'm ready to give them all the proofs they need that I'm a suitable guardian for the child, but," he added, with a touch of the boyishness that had never left him, "I want this matter settled now."

The long train pounded its way into the station at Chicago, and the nurse hurriedly put on Hope's coat and gloves and fastened the ribbons of her hood under her chin. Dr. Van Valkenberg summoned a porter.

"Take care of all these things," he said, indicating both sets of possessions with a sweep of the arm. "I shall have my hands full with my little daughter."

He gathered her into his arms as he spoke, and she nestled against his broad chest with a child's unconscious satisfaction in the strength and firmness of his clasp. The lights of the great station were twinkling in the early dusk as he stepped off the train, and the place was noisy with the greetings exchanged between the passengers and their waiting friends.

"Merry Christmas," "Merry Christmas," sounded on every side. Everybody was absorbed and excited, yet there were few who did not find time to turn a last look on a singularly attractive little child, held above the crowd in the arms of a tall man. She was laughing triumphantly as he bore her through the throng, and his heart was in his eyes as he smiled back at her.

Elizabeth G. Jordan
(1867–1947)

Elizabeth G. Jordan of Milwaukee, Wisconsin, was prominent early in the twentieth century as a critic, short-story writer, novelist, and playwright. She was a literary adviser to Harper & Brothers and a drama critic for *America*.

JOYFUL *AND* TRIUMPHANT

Senator John McCain of Arizona remembers hell on earth, as for five and a half interminable years as a prisoner of war of the North Vietnamese, he and his fellow prisoners existed from one nightmarish day to another (those who didn't die, that is).

But then came one unforgettable Christmas Eve. . . .

O come, all ye faithful, joyful and triumphant . . .

We sang little above a whisper, our eyes darting anxiously up to the barred windows for any sign of the guards.

Joyful and triumphant? Clad in tattered prisoner-of-war clothes, I looked around at the two dozen men huddled in a North Vietnamese prison cell. Lightbulbs hanging from the ceiling illuminated a gaunt and wretched group of men—grotesque caricatures of what had once been clean-shaven, superbly fit Air Force, Navy and Marine pilots and navigators.

We shivered from the damp night air and the fevers that plagued a number of us. Some men were permanently stooped from the effects of torture; others limped or leaned on makeshift crutches.

> *O come ye, o come ye to Bethlehem. Come and behold him, born the King of angels. . . .*

What a pathetic sight we were. Yet here, on this Christmas Eve in 1971, we were together for the first time, some after seven years of harrowing isolation and mistreatment at the hands of a cruel enemy.

We were keeping Christmas—the most special Christmas any of us ever would observe.

There had been Christmas services in North Vietnam in previous years, but they had been spiritless, ludicrous stage shows, orchestrated by the Vietnamese for propaganda purposes. This was *our* Christmas service, the only one we had ever been allowed to hold—though we feared that, at any moment, our captors might change their minds.

I had been designated chaplain by our senior-ranking
P.O.W. officer, Col. George "Bud" Day, USAF. As we
sang "O Come, All Ye Faithful," I looked down at the
few sheets of paper upon which I had penciled the Bible
verses that tell the story of Christ's birth.

I recalled how, a week earlier, Colonel Day had asked
the camp commander for a Bible. No, he was told,
there were no Bibles in North Vietnam. But four days
later, the camp commander had come into our commu-
nal cell to announce, "We have found one Bible in
Hanoi, and you can designate one person to copy from
it for a few minutes."

Colonel Day had requested that I perform the task.
Hastily I leafed through the worn book the Vietnamese
had placed on a table just outside our cell door in the
prison yard. I furiously copied the Christmas passages
until a guard approached and took the Bible away.

The service was simple. After saying the Lord's
Prayer, we sang Christmas carols, some of us mouthing
the words until our voices caught up with our pain-
clouded memories. Between each hymn I would read a
portion of the story of Jesus' birth.

> And the angel said unto them, Fear not: for,
> behold, I bring you good tidings of great joy,
> which shall be to all people. For unto you is born
> this day, in the city of David, a Saviour, which is
> Christ the Lord. (Luke 2:10–11, KJV)

Capt. Quincy Collins, a former choir director from
the Air Force Academy, led the hymns. At first, we
were nervous and stilted in our singing. Still burning in

our memories was the time, almost a year before, when North Vietnamese guards had burst in on our church service, beaten the three men leading the prayers, and dragged them away to confinement. The rest of us were locked away for 11 months in three-by-five-foot cells. Indeed, this Christmas service was in part a defiant celebration of the return to our regular prison in Hanoi.

And as the service progressed, our boldness increased, and the singing swelled. "O Little Town of Bethlehem," "Hark, the Herald Angels Sing," "It Came Upon the Midnight Clear." Our voices filled the cell, bound together as we shared the story of the Babe "away in a manger, no crib for a bed."

Finally it came time to sing perhaps the most beloved hymn:

> *Silent night, Holy night! All is calm, all is bright . . .*

A half dozen of the men were too sick to stand. They sat on the raised concrete sleeping platform that ran down the middle of the cell. Our few blankets were placed around the shaking shoulders of the sickest men to protect them against the cold. Even these men looked up transfixed as we sang that hymn.

> *Round yon virgin mother and child. Holy infant so*
> *tender and mild . . .*

Tears rolled down our unshaven faces. Suddenly we were two thousand years and half a world away in a village called Bethlehem. And neither war, nor torture, nor imprisonment, nor the centuries themselves had dimmed the hope born on that silent night so long before.

Sleep in heavenly peace, sleep in heavenly peace.

We had forgotten our wounds, our hunger, our pain. We raised prayers of thanks for the Christ child, for our families and homes, for our country. There was an absolutely exquisite feeling that all our burdens had been lifted. In a place designed to turn men into vicious animals, we clung to one another, sharing what comfort we had.

Some of us had managed to make crude gifts. One fellow had a precious commodity—a cotton washcloth. Somewhere he had found needle and thread and fashioned the cloth into a hat, which he gave to Bud Day. Some men exchanged dog tags. Others had used prison spoons to scratch out IOUs on bits of paper—some imaginary thing we wished another to have. We exchanged those chits with smiles and tearful thanks.

The Vietnamese guards did not disturb us. But as I looked up at the barred windows, I wished they had been looking in. I *wanted* them to see us—faithful, joyful and, yes, triumphant.

John McCain

John McCain, a former Vietnam prisoner of war and a war hero, is today a U.S. senator from Arizona.

D. J. Doig

A LOVE SONG FOR CHRISTMAS

*It had been a long, hard day in the toy department.
Dominating the stuffed-animal section was
Humphrey, a giant teddy bear. But even a red hat,
a red muffler, and spectacles hadn't been enough
to give him a home.*

Then, in came a tall man in glasses.

*T*he hands of the clock crept toward seven-thirty, and Susan Turner hoped she didn't look as tired as she felt. Her feet had become lead weights and all she could think of was the sanctuary of her apartment and the bliss of a hot bath. But there were still some late shoppers browsing about the toy department, and the sales staff at Waterson's was supposed to look cool, efficient, and cheerful, no matter what. Thank heaven, tomorrow was Christmas Eve, the last day of late closing.

But as long as the day had been, the glittering scene of the toy department still held a kind of magic for Susan. Over in the realm of dolls, woolly animals, and teddy bears, the real essence of Christmas seemed to be embodied. It was old-fashioned, she knew, but it said so much more to her than the racks of boxed games and computer toys.

Standing out, foremost among them all, was Humphrey, the giant teddy bear. He sat with a red muffler around his throat and a knitted cap on his head. He wore a red heart on his chest, like a badge, and someone with inspiration had given him a pair of spectacles so that he almost looked human and wise. Or so it seemed to Susan.

Somewhere inside Susan Turner was a little girl who still would have liked to own him. He was a friend whom she greeted in the mornings, and whom she bade good night when she switched off the lights at closing time.

By eight this evening the customers had thinned out, and Susan could take a minute to sit down by her desk and take the weight off her feet.

It was during her break that she saw the tall man in glasses, moving swiftly across the department. He didn't loiter like someone looking for ideas. He walked quickly past the shelves of mechanical toys and space-age novelties, down the aisle of stuffed animals and, without hesitating, picked up Humphrey, Susan's favorite bear, and tucked him under his arm. Held horizontally with his spectacles askew, Humphrey presented a picture of outraged dignity.

"Can you help me?" the man asked, hitching Humphrey to an upright position and setting him on the desk. "I'd like to buy this guy."

"Certainly, sir." Susan collected herself swiftly, brushing aside a slight sadness at the prospect of the bear's departure. "I think Humphrey will be glad to find a home at last."

The man, who had an attractive face, became suddenly handsome when he smiled. "Humphrey? Why do you call him that?"

"It's his name," Susan told him. "It's built in." She reached over and poked the furry stomach.

"My name is Humphrey," the bear declared in a rich baritone.

"There's a trapdoor with a battery in the small of his back," Susan explained. "He says his name every time you squeeze him."

The man produced his wallet and presented a credit card. "It's for a little girl of three. Do you think it's all right?"

Susan replied quite without the motivation of a saleswoman. "I think it's perfect. To a child that age, a big teddy will be almost real. He'll be a wonderful friend and I'm sure your little girl will love him."

"She's not my little girl. I'm her godfather." Then his eyes lit with new interest. "You seem to know a lot about children."

Susan felt the color rise in her cheeks. "Not really. It's just that when I was a little girl—" She paused, embarrassed. He wouldn't want to know about her early years in an orphanage, about the void in her life which had bred a longing for something that was strictly her own. She busied herself with the transaction and noted, when he signed, that his name was T. J. Grant.

"Don't bother trying to wrap him," he said. "I'll be taking him in a taxi." His eyes held hers a moment longer and she thought he was about to say more. Then the moment passed, and with a nod and a smile he was gone.

Susan sighed and wondered about T. J. Grant. She felt that in some odd manner her day had been turned upside down. It had been a long time since she'd met a man who radiated such a sense of warmth, but why should she have this sudden empty feeling as she watched him leave? Humphrey, of course, had gone too. The empty space where he had sat regarding her through his spectacles added to her sense of loss. But that, she told herself, was simply childish. She must be getting maudlin at the early age of twenty-five.

Still, the interlude had brought nearer the end of the working day. In half an hour she'd be on her way home. Tomorrow evening she could go to a friend's home for a family gathering. She hadn't decided yet. Her friends were always thoughtful about including her at holidays. She was grateful for that, but it wasn't like having a sense of belonging to your own family.

At last it was closing time, and Susan went mechanically through the routine of checking out. Drenching rain greeted her as she let herself out of the employees' door. There was nothing to do but wait in front of the store, in the shelter of the awning, for a taxi. On a night like this it wouldn't be easy to find one.

She'd waited five minutes when a man sprinted across the street and joined her on the steps. He was carrying something bulky wrapped in a raincoat; only when he stood panting in front of her did she recognize T. J. Grant.

He was hatless and she could see raindrops glinting in his hair. "I suppose I'm too late. I was hoping to find the store still open."

Susan tried to gather her wits. "Is anything wrong?"

He lifted one end of the raincoat to reveal the placid, furry face of Humphrey. "Well, just about everything has gone wrong. I arrived here today from Brazil, all set for an old-fashioned Christmas. The idea was to surprise my old friends who'd made me their daughter's godfather. But when I called from my hotel a few minutes ago, a stranger answered the phone. My friend is subletting his apartment. His company sent him to Canada. He'll be there for at least two years. So now the question is—what do I do with this bear?"

In spite of the rain and her fatigue, Susan was amused by his helplessness, and touched. "Well," she said after a moment's thought, "you could bring him back tomorrow. Exchange him for goods of the same value, or credit."

T. J. Grant stood there, undecided, his face a little woebegone. "I suppose so," he said. "It's just—well, it's not the money. I had this good feeling about Christmas and now it's gone flat. This teddy bear—you'll think I'm mad, but now that my plans have collapsed, I feel I want to give it to some child, somebody who'd be happy to have it."

Again, Susan was touched. "There are hospitals and orphanages, if that's what you want to do. There are ways to make it a gift, but right now it's late and—"

"I'm sorry," he broke in. "It's not your problem and you must be very tired. How long have you been in that store today?"

Susan felt herself wilting again. "Twelve hours."

Now he was really contrite. "Oh, I am sorry. Look, would you—could you possibly agree to have dinner with me, right now? You must be starving and we could talk about—about Humphrey."

Susan took five seconds to make up her mind. "All right," she said. "Thank you. I'd like that." And as if to make sure her decision was irrevocable, an empty cab pulled up to the curb in front of them.

In a moment, Susan was sitting close to T. J. Grant, and Humphrey, in his scarf and hat, leaned drunkenly against the door. His spectacles had slipped down and his brown eyes seemed to regard her with a look of profound wisdom.

By the time they arrived at the restaurant, Susan knew that T. J. stood for Thomas James and that his years in Brazil had been spent helping to build a dam. The restaurant was French and Susan liked it on sight.

She also liked the way Tom carried in the bear, as if it were the most natural thing in the world.

The head waiter smiled a welcome, apparently unmoved by the presence of Humphrey. Yes, there was a table for three, he said.

The dining room was three-quarters full, and when Humphrey was safely seated, heads began to turn in their direction.

"It's a true-life case of beauty and the beast," Tom said. "They can't help looking."

Susan grimaced. "Maybe so, but I wonder which of us looks more like the beast."

"You look beautiful," Tom said.

As the coffee and the excellent food began to restore Susan's strength and morale, she felt the strain of the long day vanish. And the longer she sat opposite T. J. Grant, the more pleased she was that it had all happened.

"About Humphrey," she said at last. "It's a little late to find a home for him tonight. But there's a children's hospital nearby. I'm sure they'd be glad to accept him. He would be ideal for the permanent toy nursery which is in use all the time."

Tom considered this. "So he wouldn't actually belong to someone?"

"Probably not. The children will be getting plenty of toys from their relatives and friends. But Humphrey— well, you would need to know some child personally to give him as a present, the way you want to."

"I see." Tom paused in thought while the waiter refilled their cups.

On an impulse, Susan told Tom about her childhood.

"I grew up in an orphanage," she said. "And we had toys, of course, but I always wanted a big teddy bear. It never happened and I suppose that's why I'm still a bit sentimental about them."

A soberness crossed Tom's face, like the shadow of something far distant. "I really don't know much about children," he said. "I only had one for two years."

Susan's eyes widened and her spirits took a surprising plunge. "You're married then?"

"I was," he said. "Several years ago. It was before I began looking for jobs in odd corners of the world. My wife and daughter were killed in a car accident."

In a flash Susan felt she understood the complexity of this man's character. Beneath the armor of everyday life lay the hunger, the loss, and the instinct to make a child happy, some real and tangible child, although it was not his own.

As life so often does, the next moment brought them both back to coping with absurdities. The waiter, nearing their table to refill their coffee cups, caught his foot, somehow, and stumbled into Humphrey's chair, knocking the bear to the floor.

Heads turned once more to their table. From below, activated by the impact, came the baritone of the bear's total vocabulary. *"My name is Humphrey."*

A ripple of laughter went through the restaurant. Humphrey was rescued, the waiter reassured, and a few minutes later Susan and Tom were out on the street again.

"That was fun," Susan said. "I'll always remember this evening." It had stopped raining and the city lights glistened on the wet pavement.

"Does it have to end here?" Tom asked. "It's early yet. Maybe we could find a good movie."

For Susan the past two hours had banished weariness and brought a vitality she had not felt for a long time. The prospect of prolonging this one pleasant evening was too strong to resist.

And so it was that they arrived, complete with bear, at the theater box office. A bored girl slid three tickets toward Tom, without raising an eyebrow at the bear.

The movie was good; a romantic thriller. During an engrossing scene, with the suspense slowly mounting, Humphrey began to topple forward, his head approaching the shoulder of the man in the seat in front.

Tom shot out a hand and caught the bear just in time—by the stomach. For one awful fraction of a second, Tom realized nothing could stop the result. The small recording inside the bear went relentlessly into action. *"My name is Humphrey."*

Those in the nearby section of the audience were jerked out of their enthrallment by the penetrating voice of the bear. One of these growling interruptions might have been only a mild distraction, but, to Susan and Tom's horror, the soundtrack kept repeating.

"My name is Humphrey. My name is Humphrey. My name is Humphrey."

Amid indignant protests, Tom grabbed Susan's arm with one hand, Humphrey's with the other. "Let's get out of here—fast!"

As they squeezed their way down the row and up the aisle to the exit, Tom muffled Humphrey's voice in the folds of his raincoat. Out on the street, they dissolved into helpless laughter.

Susan opened the flap in Humphrey's back and removed the battery. "I think he's done enough talking for tonight."

Tom aimed a right hook at Humphrey's innocent face. "He's certainly given you a hard day. I'm afraid I've been a nuisance myself."

Susan handed him the now silent bear. "I wouldn't have missed it for anything."

Another taxi took them to the entrance of Susan's apartment. When Tom got out and stood with her on the sidewalk, she was aware that something was about to end that she would find hard to forget. This chance meeting with T. J. Grant, this casual but memorable evening, had now reached its inevitable conclusion.

"Well, good luck finding a home for Humphrey," she said. "I suppose you'll be moving on somewhere."

"Nowhere to move to," he replied. "No family now, and all I have in this town is a bank account, a lawyer, and a desk in my firm's head office. But right now, all I need is sleep."

She saw with concern that his face was pale and behind his glasses his eyes were heavy with fatigue. It suddenly hit her that only this morning he had flown in from South America. A wave of sadness brought a tightness to her throat. "Good-bye, then. Perhaps you'll let me know what happens to Humphrey."

Barely ten minutes later, she was preparing a hot drink when the sound of the doorbell made her start with surprise. When she opened the door, there was T. J. Grant, holding the bear.

By now she was getting used to the unexpected.

Without losing her poise, she said calmly, "Come in and have some coffee. I'm just making it."

He stood inside the door. "I had to come back," he said. "I stopped the cab because something suddenly dawned on me. I know now who I want to give Humphrey to. He's yours, Susan. After this evening, I couldn't give him to anyone else."

Susan's heart began to thump wildly. She put Humphrey down tenderly in the nearest chair, but it was some seconds before she was able to speak. "I'd love to have him. But if I do take him, he'll always be partly yours."

Tom came and stood beside her. It seemed natural that he take her hand. "If I have a share in Humphrey, could that include a share in you?"

For Susan, the room, previously empty and lifeless, appeared to sparkle and come alive. "Well, for a start, come here tomorrow when you've had enough sleep. We'll celebrate Humphrey's homecoming. How about that?"

Tom gave a sigh of relief. "I've been wondering if I could survive Christmas in a strange hotel. But Humphrey has solved everything."

He punched the bear's midriff, but this time Humphrey said nothing. He only stared ahead with his soft brown eyes and seemed to smile secretly.

D. J. Doig

David T. Doig was a native of Scotland and died there in 1990. He was an extremely prolific writer, and his stories have been published all over the world.

Jewell Johnson

MERRY CHRISTMAS,
MR. KEENE

The whole town wondered why the rich Mr. Keene never went to church anymore and why he disliked Christmas so. Why should the children trudge through blowing snow all the way up the hill just to sing carols to him? He wouldn't appreciate it.

They did it anyway. And sure enough . . .

*T*hey trudged down the path, the five of them, their heavy overshoes crunching softly on the snow-packed road. At the corner, they stopped and stood under the street light. Bobby, the oldest, pulled the woolen muffler away from his face.

"Where should we go now?" he asked.

For a moment, no one spoke.

"How about Mr. Keene's?" his sister, Marilyn, asked.

Peering into the shadowy darkness, she could see the Keene mansion looming on a hill half a mile from where they stood.

The others were silent. They had sung Christmas carols for Widow Sorvik, old Mr. Bengston and others in the neighborhood. It had never occurred to them to venture beyond—and certainly not to sing for the proprietor of Keene's Mercantile and Dry Goods store.

"It's pretty far up there," said Joanie, a tall eleven-year-old. She studied the winding lane to the mansion.

"Yeah, and Mr. Keene's hard of hearing," Earl chimed in.

"Besides, he never goes to church," Bobby added. "He doesn't even like Christmas carols."

The children had heard their parents speculate on the reasons why Mr. Keene didn't darken the church door. Some said it was because he was too deaf to hear the preacher. Others thought that Northridge's only millionaire was excused from ordinary things like churchgoing.

As the children pondered whether to go home or brave the long road to the Keene mansion, Mary Ann's high-pitched voice pierced the night air. "If we sing carols for him, we can invite him to the Christmas pageant." She patted her red mittens together, pleased to have come up with the idea.

The children's pageant was the highlight of the town's Christmas celebration. Angie Atwood, the director, planned an elaborate presentation with angels, wise men, shepherds, and a children's choir in white robes.

"We want the whole town to be here Christmas Eve," Angie had said at Saturday's practice. "It will be the most wonderful Christmas pageant ever."

As the children talked, the wind blew sharply, gnawing through their heavy coats and whirling powdery snow at their feet.

"Let's go sing carols for Mr. Keene and invite him to the pageant," Bobby said. "Miss Angie would like that."

The Keene mansion stood apart from the town. It was situated on a five-acre tract, surrounded by giant cottonwoods, elms and maple trees. The huge branches, now bare, swayed and creaked in the night. Hedges loomed like shadowy, white mounds in the pale starlight, and banks of snow stood like sentinels on either side of the narrow lane.

When the children approached the mansion, they noticed that only a few lights were on. One window where a light shone was on the second floor. The shade was pulled partway down.

"Do you think he'll hear us?" Earl asked, raising his eyes to the window.

"His housekeeper, Mrs. Rustad, will," Joanie answered.

They stood knee-deep in snow and sang, "O little town of Bethlehem, how still we see thee lie . . ."

When the last note faded, they waited, expecting the shade to spring up.

It didn't move.

"Let's try 'Joy to the World,'" Bobby said, as he stomped his feet to keep warm. "We can get loud on that one."

They strained their voices, all the while craning their necks for a glimpse of Mr. Keene at the window.

"He can't hear us," Joanie sighed.

Not easily discouraged, they filled their lungs with frigid air and sang "Silent Night."

The window shade didn't even quiver.

"It's no use," Earl said. "He's too deaf."

Like battle-worn soldiers, they turned to find their way back.

"Children! Children, would you like to come inside and sing for Mr. Keene?"

Mrs. Rustad appeared in the shadows, hugging a pink sweater around her checkered housedress.

"Would you like to come in?" she repeated.

"Yes! Yes!" they shouted.

Hopping over the snow drifts like arctic kangaroos, the carolers pushed their way toward the back entrance of the mansion.

Mrs. Rustad led them into a large, heated room. "Wait here," she said.

Looking around, the children saw Mr. Keene's eight-buckle overshoes standing on the green linoleum. A table and chair stood against one wall.

The door swung open, and Mr. Keene stepped into the room. No one spoke. To pass Mr. Keene in his

store was one thing; to see him in his house was quite
another.

"You came to sing for me?" he asked. His stern, gray
eyes swept over the children.

Five heads nodded.

"What are your names?"

He pointed a finger at Bobby.

"Bobby Carlson. This is my little sister. She's seven."
Bobby nodded toward Marilyn.

"Speak louder, children," Mrs. Rustad said. "Mr.
Keene is hard of hearing."

"Earl . . . Earl . . . ," a little boy repeated, unable to
remember his last name.

"Barry," Joanie announced. "And I'm Joanie
Pearson. This is Mary Ann Swanson." Joanie pointed a
blue mitten in Mary Ann's direction. "She's five."

Mr. Keene adjusted his hearing aid. He leaned on the
table with his left hand, put his right hand on his hip
and fixed his eyes on the linoleum.

It was time to sing.

"Joy to the world! The Lord is come . . ." they sang.
The hope-filled words warmed the chilly room. Softly
they sang "Silent Night" and then "Hark! The Herald
Angels Sing."

As the music faded, Mrs. Rustad wiped her eyes. Mr.
Keene cleared his throat and shifted his feet.

"Aren't you going to ask him?" Mary Ann's shrill
voice broke the silence. She looked at Bobby.

"It was your idea," he retorted.

"Children, what do you want to ask Mr. Keene?"
Mrs. Rustad asked.

"About the pageant," Mary Ann said defiantly, as if Mrs. Rustad should know.

"What is this about?" Mr. Keene looked from Mrs. Rustad to Bobby, then back at the housekeeper.

"I don't know," she said. "I don't know," she repeated with a shrug.

"The Christmas pageant, sir," Bobby said. "At the church on Christmas Eve. Will you come?"

"What?" Mr. Keene asked, a puzzled look on his face. "What's Christmas Eve?" He cupped his hand over his right ear as Mrs. Rustad leaned closer.

"The church is having a pageant on Christmas Eve. The children are inviting you."

Mr. Keene dropped his hand from his ear and laughed. "You want me at the church?" His eyes swept over them, and he shifted his feet.

"It's very special, Mr. Keene," Mary Ann said in her shrill voice. "It's Jesus' birthday, and I'm going to be an angel!"

"Oh . . . how sweet," Mrs. Rustad murmured.

"I don't go to church," Mr. Keene said. "Not anymore. I used to when I was your age. But not since . . ."

His voice trailed off, and he ran his hand over his head. "I'm sorry, miss."

Joanie's voice broke the silence. "Merry Christmas, Mr. Keene."

"Merry Christmas," the others said as they filed out the door.

"Yes, well. Merry Christmas to you," Mr. Keene said. But the children noticed his eyes didn't meet their gaze.

A thin, white moon came out as the children started down the lane. With faces bowed into their woolen mufflers, they plodded along in silence.

Finally Bobby spoke.

"Maybe the old pageant isn't so important after all," he said slowly.

"Bobby Carlson!" Joanie exclaimed. "Not important? What do you mean by that?"

"Well, if a millionaire like Mr. Keene doesn't want to come, why have it? I mean, he knows more than all of us put together. And he never goes to church. Never! And he's smart enough to make a million dollars. Maybe . . ."

"But Miss Angie goes," Mary Ann interrupted.

"What does she know? She just works at McLean's Drug Store. She doesn't own a store like Mr. Keene. Oh, I'm not saying we shouldn't have the pageant. But why get so excited about it?"

"But it *is* important," Marilyn said. "The angels, the wise men, the shepherds and baby Jesus. It *is* important! I know it is!"

"Anyway, what does Miss Angie know?" Earl asked, coming to Bobby's defense. "She's just an old lady."

"She is not!" the girls shouted.

"She's the best person in the whole world, Earl Barry," Joanie said.

"Then why isn't she a millionaire?" Bobby asked.

Joanie had no answer. She knew there was a good reason why Mr. Keene was a millionaire while Miss Angie only worked in the drug store, but at the moment, she couldn't come up with an answer.

❊ ❊ ❊

After the children were dismissed from rehearsal, Miss Angie; Freda Nordquist, the choir director; and Lillian Borg, the pianist, sank into the front pew.

"I hope next Saturday's practice goes smoother," Miss Angie sighed. "Did it seem to either of you that some of the children were . . . disinterested?"

"Bobby Carlson, for one," Freda stated matter-of-factly. "That child is usually so excited about being a shepherd, so anxious to please. He seemed . . . listless." Her voice hung on the last word.

"Exactly!" Miss Angie exclaimed. "That's just the word—listless."

She pulled a bright blue beret over her gray curls and reached for her coat.

"I hope he's not coming down with something. Goodbye, ladies. I'll see you tomorrow in church."

As Miss Angie stepped outside the church, she noticed a group of children at the bottom of the stairs. One of them had his back toward her.

"The pageant isn't so important," Bobby Carlson's boisterous voice floated to the top of the steps. "Heck, Mr. Keene won't be there. And he knows a lot 'cause he's made a million dollars and runs a big store. Why get excited about an old pageant? Why invite anyone? I asked Mr. Keene to come, but he doesn't think it's important enough to show his face. So there!"

Bobby held the others spellbound.

"Bobby Carlson!" Miss Angie's voice snapped like a whip.

She quickly spanned the ten steps to the children.

"Bobby, who told you the pageant isn't important? Who said that?"

She pushed her finger into his chest, her blue eyes flashing.

"I never said that," Bobby gasped, backing away. "No, Miss Angie, I never said anything about the pageant not being important."

"Bobby, someone put that idea in your head. Who was it?"

She turned to the others, searching each face.

"Mr. Keene did," a high-pitched voice said. It was Mary Ann.

"When Bobby asked him to come, he said he didn't go to church. Never!"

Bobby held his breath; his eyes were ready to pop. He wanted to stop the voice. He wanted to shout or run—anything to get away from the hurt in Miss Angie's eyes and the anger in her voice.

Joanie raised her hand. "Some of us kids went to sing Christmas carols for Mr. Keene, and we invited him to the pageant, because you said to invite everybody."

"You went to his house?" Miss Angie tried to appear calm.

"Yeah, and he said he used to go to church. But he doesn't anymore. And then Bobby said that if a millionaire like Mr. Keene doesn't want to come to the pageant, maybe it's not important."

Miss Angie folded her arms and rocked on her heels.

"Hmmm. We'll see about this. Bobby, Mary Ann, Joanie. Who else sang carols for Mr. Keene?"

Earl and Marilyn reluctantly raised their hands.

"Come along," Miss Angie commanded with a wave of her hand.

It was two weeks before Christmas. The crowd in Keene's Mercantile was larger than usual. Farmers and their wives came to town to trade eggs and cream for groceries, Christmas candy, and gifts.

Curious eyes turned to watch Angie Atwood and the children march past the men's hat rack, the three-way mirror and the men's overalls, up the steps to Mr. Keene's office.

Miss Angie leaned into the office window and announced, "I'd like to speak with Mr. Keene."

Ruby White, the secretary, rose slowly.

"I'll . . . I'll see if he's available, Miss Angie," she said.

Angie drummed her fingers on the window ledge, while the children, white-faced and silent, stood nearby. Then she jumped, startled by a gruff voice behind her. Mr. Keene stepped from the shadows.

"You want to see me, Angie?" His eyes were steel-cold, and he wore his gray hat.

Miss Angie folded her gloved hands. "Zebedee Keene, I've left you alone for twenty-five years."

"That was not my choosing," he snapped.

"But do I understand, Zebedee," she continued, "you told these children that the Christmas pageant and attendance at church are not important?"

"Did I say that?" His gray eyes stared hawk-eyed at the children. They shook their heads. It seemed to them that Mr. Keene's hearing had improved considerably.

"But you did say you're not coming to the pageant, didn't you, Zebedee?"

"Yes, but . . ."

"It's the same thing. These children concluded that when the proprietor of Keene's Mercantile, the biggest enterprise in Northridge, doesn't plan to show up at the pageant after receiving a special invitation, it's the same as saying Christmas, the pageant and church aren't important. Isn't that what you children thought? Isn't it?"

Five heads nodded in unison.

"See! Now, I want you to tell these children that the Christmas pageant is important and that you'll be there."

Miss Angie rocked on her heels, her eyes never leaving Mr. Keene's face.

"Confound it, Angie!" he exclaimed. "I'll promise no such thing. I haven't been in church since . . ." Mr. Keene shifted his feet. "No, I can't make that promise," he said.

"Very well, Zebedee. We'll leave it like this: If Christmas is important, we'll see you in church on Christmas Eve. If not, well . . ." Miss Angie's voice trailed off.

She took a deep breath. "It's up to you, Zebedee. What the children of this community become is in your hands. Come along, children. Good day, Zebedee."

"Now see here, Angie," Mr. Keene thundered.

He was left standing alone.

"Confound it," he muttered stomping his foot. "Confound Angie Atwood!"

❄ ❄ ❄

Bobby and Earl, dressed in burlap robes, sat squeezed between the wise men and angels in the front row. It was the last rehearsal.

"Are you sick or somethin'?" Earl asked, glancing at Bobby.

"No. Why?"

"You look kinda funny."

"Earl, we've got to get Mr. Keene here tomorrow night," Bobby said. "Can't you get your dad to ask him?"

"Naw, he won't. Dad told me Mr. Keene hasn't been in church for twenty-five years."

Miss Angie interrupted.

"Children, quiet. We're going to begin practice. Please take your places."

Joanie leaned over the back of the pew and whispered in Bobby's ear, "Miss Angie looks real pale, doesn't she?"

After the children were dismissed, Miss Angie said, "Freda, I'll bring safety pins and one more set of angel wings. Can you think of anything else we might be forgetting?"

"No, everything's in order," Freda said. "Are you feeling well, Angie? You look a bit peaked."

"I'll be fine once the pageant is over. It's this last-minute worry. I do hope the weather stays nice and the children stay well."

"Go home, Angie. Make a cup of tea and put your feet up," Lillian said. "Freda and I will get the costumes ready for tomorrow night."

Outside, the five children huddled together and watched as Miss Angie walked away from the church.

"It's kinda sad," Joanie said. "A lot of people are coming, but not Mr. Keene. I sure wish there was a way

. . . Oh, I forgot my mittens. Wait here. My mom won't like it if I lose another pair."

Inside the church, Joanie walked to the front pew. She heard voices coming from the room beyond the sanctuary.

"Miss Angie takes things too hard," Joanie heard Freda Nordquist say. "I'm afraid she's thinking about Zebedee Keene."

"Did she really jilt him?" Lillian Borg asked.

"Yes, the very day of the wedding. Mr. Keene was left standing at the altar. You never saw a man so in love as Zebedee Keene. And Angie found out after she eloped with Howard Atwood that she'd married a drunk. Then it was too late."

"Now that Howard's dead, do you suppose there's a chance for her and Mr. Keene?" Lillian asked.

"Utterly impossible," Freda said. "Mr. Keene is all business now. All he cares about is money. But sometimes, I think Angie still cares for him."

Freda sighed.

"Ready to go, Lillian?"

Joanie grabbed her mittens and raced outside. "You found them," Earl said.

"What?"

"Your mittens—what you went into the church for," Bobby said.

"Listen, you guys," Joanie said. "Miss Angie and Mr. Keene, a long time ago, were supposed to get married, but she married Mr. Atwood instead. That's why Mr. Keene won't go to church. Miss Angie left him standing there on their wedding day." She gasped for breath. "And we're going to get them back together. Okay?"

"But how?" Earl asked.

"That's what we're going to figure out," Joanie said.

"That'll be easy," Marilyn boasted. "I read it once in a book. We'll write a letter to Mr. Keene and apologize for not marrying him and sign Miss Atwood's name. Easy as pie."

"But that's against the law to sign somebody else's name. Forestry or something," Earl said.

"Forgery," Bobby corrected him. "No, that won't work. We'll have to think of another way."

❄ ❄ ❄

On Sunday night, chaos reigned in the church choir room as the children scrambled to get into their costumes and choir robes.

"Children, please," Freda Nordquist pleaded, clapping her hands to get their attention. "Please, quiet down."

The din only increased.

Lillian Borg was assembling the children in the choir when Miss Angie rushed to her side.

"Where are Earl and Bobby?" she asked.

"What? Is someone missing, Angie?"

"Two of the boys—Earl and Bobby," she said. "My shepherds."

"Have you asked Bobby's sister?"

Miss Angie, in a red dress, her cheeks pink, pushed through the children to where Marilyn stood in a white robe and gold halo.

"They're coming. Don't worry, Miss Angie. They'll be here," Marilyn said.

At 7:25 P.M., the children stood in a straight line in the church foyer, ready to march into the sanctuary. Miss Angie stood by the door, with burlap robes draped over one arm and shepherds' crooks in her hands.

"Oh, what will we do? Marilyn, are you sure they're coming?" she asked in a whisper. "What will I do if they don't come? What will a Christmas pageant be without shepherds?"

❄ ❄ ❄

Northridge's main street was deserted that night except for two figures moving quickly in the semidarkness.

"We've got to hurry, Earl. We can't be late," Bobby said. "And it's a long way up to Mr. Keene's house. Hey, isn't that his car by the mercantile?"

Even with a light snow falling, Bobby could see the outline of a car parked by the store's side entrance.

"Yeah, sure looks like it," Earl said. "We won't even have to go to his house. But do you think he'll hear us?"

At the mercantile door, they pushed their faces close to the glass. A green shade obscured their view, but in the small space where the shade and door did not meet, they saw light coming from Mr. Keene's office.

"Remember, you pound on the door, and I'll do the talking," Bobby said. He took a long, deep breath to quiet the thumping of his heart.

"Okay," Earl said.

Bobby leaned heavily on Earl's shoulder, almost pushing him over.

"Go easy," Earl said as he began pounding his fist on the door.

After a few seconds, Earl stopped. "My hand's getting tired," he said.

"Keep knocking," Bobby said. "He's bound to hear us." Earl started pounding on the door again.

"Knock harder."

"I can't."

At that moment, the green shade parted, and Mr. Keene's face appeared in the window.

"What in tarnation?" they heard him grumble as he searched his coat pocket for a key.

With one click, the door swung open, and Mr. Keene loomed before them. He was dressed in a gray hat and suit and wore his eight-buckle overshoes.

"What is the meaning of this?" he asked, glaring down at the two figures on the snowy street.

"Talk," Earl hissed, poking Bobby with his elbow.

"Mr. Keene, we're in trouble. We need help," Bobby panted. "We're supposed to be at the church, but I fell. I think I broke something, and we're supposed to be shepherds. Could you give us a lift to the church, please? Could you, Mr. Keene?"

"Think you broke a leg, do you?" Mr. Keene spoke pensively. "What you need to do is go home."

"There's no one at my house. My folks are at the church. Besides, Earl here needs to be in the pageant. We can't disappoint Miss Angie."

"Miss Angie, eh?"

"Yeah, we need to get Earl to the church."

"Get in the car, boys. I'll lock up."

"I don't know if I can walk, sir," Bobby said.

He took a step, winced and grabbed Mr. Keene's arm.

At the church, Earl and Mr. Keene labored up the steps supporting Bobby between them. They came through the door just as the last wise man started up the aisle.

"Earl! Bobby!" Miss Angie exclaimed. "Why . . . why, Zebedee, you came!" For a moment she forgot the burlap robes on her arm.

"Earl, Bobby, quickly, get into these." She began slipping the rough robe over Bobby's head.

"He can't. He can't be a shepherd, Angie," Mr. Keene said. "His leg is hurt. It may be only a sprain, but I don't think it's a good idea to walk on it."

Miss Angie gazed into Mr. Keene's gray eyes and held out the robe. He caught his breath and took a step back.

"No," he whispered.

"Zebedee, please. Just this once," she pleaded.

"Confound it, I haven't been in this church for twenty-five years, and when I come, you make a fool of me—every time."

"Shh, Zebedee. People will hear you," she said softly.

❄ ❄ ❄

The light grew dim, and the choir began to sing "Silent Night" as two shepherds started down the aisle.

At the manger the smallest shepherd knelt in the hay. The taller one stood with bowed head, his staff gleaming in the light of the star.

"And there were in the same country shepherds abiding in the field," the narrator said. "And the glory of the Lord shone round about them. . . ."

The tall shepherd sighed deeply as if releasing an unseen burden. The small shepherd turned, and before he knew what he did, Earl reached up and took Mr. Keene by the hand. As if by a signal, the angel next to Mr. Keene grasped his other hand. The wise men set down their gifts and joined hands with the angels until a ring of heavenly and earthly beings encircled the manger.

"O, come let us adore Him," the choir sang.

When the pageant ended, parents filed past Miss Angie. "Great program, Angie," Earl's father said.

"You certainly know how to get these kids to perform," Joanie's mother said.

Out of the corner of her eye, Angie noticed a lone figure standing apart from the crowd.

"Miss Angie, it was wonderful." Bobby's mother grasped her hand. "What you do with the children is amazing."

"Thank you, Mrs. Carlson. How's Bobby's leg?"

"Leg? I didn't . . ."

"I'm sorry, Miss Angie," Bobby said, eyes downcast. "My leg's not really hurt. It was the only way I could think of to get Mr. Keene here."

Angie looked at Bobby sternly. "I think you have some explaining to do—to your mother and to Mr. Keene. But not now, not now," she said in an odd tone of voice.

After the crowd thinned, Angie walked toward Mr. Keene.

"Zebedee, how can I ever thank you. . . ."

Something in his eyes silenced her.

"It was at this very spot," he said, choking on the words. "I stood right here. Only it was June then, twenty-five years ago."

Angie turned ashen, remembering.

"I vowed I'd never forgive you, Angie, and I meant . . ."

"Yoo-hoo Angie, I'll give you a lift home," Freda said. "Oh, I'm sorry. I didn't mean to interrupt. I'll just wait in the car. I don't want you walking alone. . . ."

"She has a ride," Mr. Keene said.

"I do?" Angie looked bewildered. "I mean, no, I don't need a ride. The walk will do me good after all this excitement."

"Well, so long, Angie."

Freda nodded at Mr. Keene. "Good evening."

Zebedee Keene and Angie Atwood stared at each other. Angie dropped her gaze.

"I was so ashamed afterward. I couldn't come and tell you I was sorry. I couldn't bear to face you." She pushed a curl away from her face. "I know you've never forgiven me because what I did was unforgivable. I know that. But I want you to know I was sorry. The very next day I was sorry. I'm sorry now."

Angie stopped and watched as Mr. Keene fumbled in his vest pocket.

"It's here someplace," he said. She gasped as she saw a small object glisten in his hand.

"The ring," he said, a crooked smile on his face. "I kept the ring. I've carried it with me. And if you'll . . ." He stumbled over the words. "Confound it, Angie, what I'm trying to say is, will you take the ring back? Will you be my wife?"

Her shoulders shook as tears fell on her dress, making dark stains.

"Get your coat, Angie," he said softly.

Outside, five youngsters watched from a distance. They saw Mr. Keene brush the snow from the car and hold the door open as Angie Atwood got in.

As Mr. Keene and Angie drove away, Joanie sighed.

"I guess we can go home."

"I'll race you!" Earl shouted.

Laughing, Marilyn and Joanie started after him.

"Hey, wait for me," Mary Ann shrieked, slipping on the icy road.

"Let's sing," Bobby yelled.

"Joy to the world! The Lord is come," he sang, waving his hands in the air.

"And heav'n and nature sing," the others joined him. "And heav'n and nature sing . . ."

The words echoed through the town's streets and alleys in the still night.

Jewell Johnson

Jewell Johnson of Fountain Hills, Arizona, writes for contemporary family and inspirational magazines.

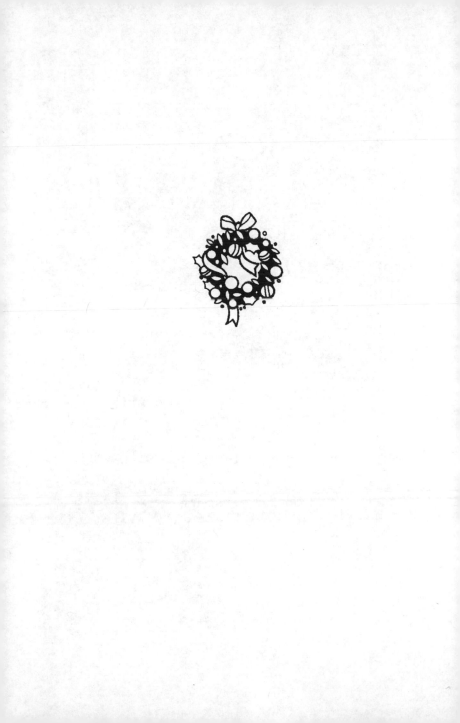

Ruth Langland Holberg

A SONG IS BORN

"I wish we had some new music. Doesn't anyone ever compose songs nowadays? Must we always have Handel and Bach?"

This story has been retold in many ways. This is one of the very special ones.

*A*nna Lisa Mohr laid away the carved rolling pin. "Finished already with the *springerle,* Anna Lisa?" asked her mother, surveying the array of Christmas cookies.

"Yes, Mother. And now I go to choir practice."

She stumbled over a chair in her haste to get her woolen shawl from the chest.

"Careful, Anna Lisa. Your father is writing his Christmas sermon and needs a quiet house; and besides, the baby has just dropped off to sleep. He cries so much these days because of the new teeth that are coming through."

Softly Anna Lisa closed the door and stepped out into the snowy afternoon. After a few minutes' walking she met Hildegarde and Johann Hartz, who had made a long trip down the mountainside on skis. Together they went into the church.

❄ ❄ ❄

The organist was Franz Gruber. He was also the schoolmaster in that village of Oberndorf tucked away in the Austrian mountains. Franz Gruber had a way with young people, and as soon as he stepped before them and told them what they were to sing he had their attention.

Johann whispered to Anna Lisa when the number was finished, "I wish we had some new music. Doesn't anyone ever compose songs nowadays? Must we always have Handel and Bach?"

Anna Lisa turned a shocked face.

"There isn't anything finer than their works. Herr Gruber says so and he should know. Don't you remember hearing that when he was a boy in Unterweizberg his schoolmaster gave him lessons secretly at night?"

Johann shook his head in surprise. "Why were the lessons secret?"

"You see, his father was a linen weaver, as his family had been before him; and of course his son was to be a weaver too, even though he wanted to be a musician. Why, as a child Herr Gruber even made little blocks of wood and stuck them in the cracks of the wall and pretended they were organ keys so he could practice finger exercises on them! One day their schoolmaster was suddenly taken ill and could not play the organ. It was an important service with all the people in church, and Herr Gruber—he was only twelve then—jumped to the organ bench and played the entire service from memory!" Her rosy face was lighted with the amazing story.

"Yes?" Johann was impressed. He looked at the threadbare man. "But what did his father do about that?" he asked.

"The townspeople made such a hero of him that his father bought an old piano and allowed his son to take regular lessons. Besides, he let him study to become a schoolmaster. His father knew then that he would be better at that than weaving."

Anna Lisa gave her attention to the prelude for sopranos.

❄ ❄ ❄

It was almost Christmas. Frau Mohr rocked the cradle of her youngest child. When he had fallen asleep, she started off to do some holiday marketing.

Pastor Mohr was finishing his sermon at last. It seemed as if he would never get it ready. All at once small Hans sent up a lusty cry.

Pastor Mohr shook his head in despair and went to the cradle and rocked it. But Hans kept on crying until his father took him in his arms and walked the floor. With the Christmas sermon in his mind and the picture of that faraway night when a babe was born in a manger, Pastor Mohr tried to comfort Hans with some verses that he made up as he went along.

"You like the verses, Hansi?" murmured the father. "They make you forget your teething troubles, eh?"

He crooned more softly, and the fuzzy head nodded on his shoulder. Finally he laid the sleeping boy in his cradle and tiptoed to his study. The verses kept running in his head as if they had a tune. He wrote them on a sheet of paper and wished he could write the music for them that he had heard in his heart.

The Christmas sermon was finished when Frau Mohr returned.

Anna Lisa came to her father's study with a cup of hot milk. She saw the paper before him. "Have you written a poem, Father?"

Absent-mindedly he glanced at the paper. "Ah, yes, read it, Daughter." He drank the milk gratefully. When Anna Lisa finished reading it, she looked at her father with starry eyes. "Oh, if it had music! It would be a Christmas song for the choir to sing tomorrow night!"

"Tomorrow night!" He was startled from his dreaming of the music.

"Oh, yes, Father!" she pleaded. "Johann said no one

ever composes new songs nowadays, and I know Herr Gruber could do it!"

"He could, but it is too late now."

She took her father's hand urgently. "We practice tonight, and Herr Gruber could compose a melody this afternoon. Don't I see him do it in school? Has not Mother made a basket of cookies for me to take Frau Gruber this afternoon? Come with me. He will make a song of the poem."

Somehow Anna Lisa persuaded her father that he must go at once to ask Franz Gruber to set the poem to music.

The pastor read the poem to the organist. He could see the musician's eyes grow keen. At once Herr Gruber seized paper and commenced to make notes of music on it. In less than an hour it was finished.

Anna Lisa begged, "Could the choir keep it a secret and surprise the congregation tomorrow night with a new song?"

Herr Gruber laughed. "How like a girl! But I guess we all like Christmas surprises. I know my wife and I will enjoy the gift of cookies you surprised us with. It shall be as you wish."

At choir practice that evening every child and young person agreed to keep the new song a secret. Johann was particularly pleased to have something different to sing, but he wondered if the song would last as long as a Handel or Bach piece.

"Maybe it will last as long," nodded Anna Lisa wisely.

The melody was simple, and after an hour's practice the choir knew it well. It seemed almost at once to become a part of them.

❄ ❄ ❄

On Christmas Eve the old familiar music rang out jubilantly. Then an air of suspense suddenly took possession of the people, for the choir was looking on them with shining faces. People exchanged puzzled looks. Franz Gruber began a soft prelude never heard before. After a few bars the young voices took up the melody, so reverently that a choking sensation was in every throat.

> *Silent night! Holy night!*
> *All is calm, all is bright.*
> *'Round yon virgin mother and Child!*
> *Holy Infant, so tender and mild;*
> *Sleep in heavenly peace,*
> *Sleep in heavenly peace.*

The girls' voices wove through the verse with a lullaby for the Holy Infant. The boys' clear, soaring tones were like angelic flutes bringing peace to the congregation. They sang on.

> *Silent night! Holy night!*
> *Shepherds quake at the sight!*
> *Glories stream from heaven afar,*
> *Heav'nly hosts sing Alleluia;*
> *Christ, the Savior, is born,*
> *Christ, the Savior, is born.*

Again the choir took up the hushing theme and lifted to the high notes with delicate grace before they reached the last words.

Silent night! Holy night!
Son of God, love's pure light.
Radiant beams from Thy holy face,
With the dawn of redeeming grace;
Jesus, Lord, at Thy birth,
Jesus, Lord, at Thy birth.

Though the singing had ended, the congregation felt the melody was carried on and on through invisible spaces that reached to the very throne of heaven. Many brushed away their tears of emotion, and many bowed their heads in solemn gratitude for the gift of music that the young people had given them that Christmas Eve in 1818.

Ruth Langland Holberg

Ruth Langland Holberg wrote for family and inspirational magazines during the first half of the twentieth century.

SANTA CLAUS IS KINDNESS

This isn't a story about Santa Claus at all. It's really about Nancy, a young woman who had lost all faith in goodness, constancy, and enduring values—in marriage itself, because her father and mother left each other. Because their love failed to last.

And that's the reason Simon decided not to marry her.

*C*hristmas was only two days away when Nancy Spaulding discovered that she was in love with Simon Meriweather. The idea was not new to her, but hitherto she had fought it off. Simon was something of a prig, and she had known him all her life, a combination which does not always make for romance. Yet because she had known him throughout the years, Nancy forgave the priggishness. Or rather, she held that it had its origin in high-mindedness.

To Nancy's crowd, high-mindedness smacked of mid-Victorian ideals and all the stodgy virtues, but Nancy, defending him, declared that Simon's virtues set him apart.

"The rest of you are so standardized," she told Crane Mawson.

"If you mean me," Crane flung back at her, "you can stop right there. I am not standardized. My vices are my own, and Simon is welcome to his virtues."

"You would say that, of course, with all your money."

"Money has nothing to do with it."

"It has. You think I'll forgive your faults for the sake of your fortune."

Crane flushed. "Don't be brutal."

"Well, you shouldn't say such things of Simon."

It was in that moment of her defense of him that Nancy had come to know her heart. She wanted Simon, priggishness and all, for her husband. And she meant to have him.

He hadn't asked her yet, but that was a mere detail. He would if she wanted him to. He loved her. By every sign known to astute femininity she was certain of it. He didn't quite approve of her, but in spite of her faults he loved her.

The reason he didn't approve of her was that she was selfish and shallow. Only a few nights ago he had said:

"What's the matter with you, Nan? Life is something more than cakes and ale."

"Is it?"

"You know it is. You were a lovely little girl. You're lovely now, but you're slipping."

That was Simon—always telling you the truth about yourself. And, strange to say, Nancy found it refreshing. There were enough people to flatter you, but when Simon praised or blamed, it meant something. Now and then he admitted a mistake, but when he was right, he held to it.

"I hate that crowd you're so keen about."

"Crane Mawson's?"

"Yes."

"But it's your crowd, too, Simon."

"In a way. But I don't fall for a lot of it. And you do. Snap out of it, darling."

"Out of what?"

"Well, you used to believe in things—"

He had stopped there, but she had known what he wanted to say. That the child Nancy had had faith and hope and courage. And now faith and hope and courage were dead words, for when she was fourteen, her life had changed. It was then that her father and mother had come to a parting of the ways. A divorce had followed, and after that Nancy had lived six months with one parent and six months with the other. Every other

Christmas she spent with her father, who had married again and who gave wild parties. The alternate Christmas she spent with her mother, who had also married again and who also gave wild parties.

Nancy hated it all. Still, a mother was a mother, and a father, a father. She defended them savagely, saying things to Simon about love and marriage that she didn't mean, and saying them because of an exaggerated sense of loyalty which made her rush to the defense of that which was not defensible.

This Christmas she was to spend neither with her father, who was cruising in the Caribbean, nor her mother, who was cruising in the Mediterranean. As her Christmas celebration was therefore left to her own planning, Nancy thought a great deal about it. A lot of people had asked her to dine, but she had put them off. She had hoped Simon would ask her, but now it was too late. He lived alone with his father, and they were to spend the Christmas season with Simon's grandmother, who had an old-fashioned house in the hills of Vermont. That left Nancy definitely out. There was no reason why she should feel left out, but she did.

Feeling somewhat depressed, therefore, yet with something of hope in her heart, she decided to go downtown and do the last of her Christmas shopping. She took a bus part of the way, then walked to the shops. It was snowing, and she liked the snow. She liked, too, the hurrying crowds, the wreaths in the windows, the Santa Clauses on the corners. She dropped a dollar in the Christmas kettle of the Salvation Army lassie who teetered on her cold toes and smiled at

Nancy from under her demure bonnet. Nancy smiled back.

It had been something of a wrench to give that dollar. She had a generous allowance from her father, but she had spent it all and had mortgaged future remittances. She had charge accounts everywhere, but cash was short, and she would have to conserve it until her Christmas gift checks came in.

Of course she might borrow from Simon. She had often done it, and there had never been any embarrassment about those borrowings.

"Be a good pal," she would say, "and lend me a few dollars."

And Simon would ask, "How much?" And sometimes it had been as much as a hundred dollars.

Simon had always been a dear about everything, and they had been such friends. When she was five and he was twelve, he had given her his first Christmas present. And he had taught her a song. Nancy, looking in the windows as she passed, was seeing beyond them a rich and glowing room where she sat in a big chair by the fire, and Simon, a curly-headed lad of twelve, stood before her beating time:

> *A ship, a ship a-sailing,*
> *A-sailing on the sea,*
> *And it was deeply laden*
> *With pretty things for me. . . .*

It was not exactly a Christmas song, but they had sung it together every Christmas and called it their song. They would sing it together tonight, out under the stars if the snow stopped; and if the snow did not stop, they would sing it anyway.

She was to see him at Crane Mawson's. Crane had a big country place up the Hudson and was giving a party. They would skate on the pond and eat out-of-doors at midnight, with fires blazing and things cooking over the coals. Nancy was to go in Crane's car, for Simon, being more than usually busy before the holidays, would be late. Simon was twenty-seven and a member of his father's law firm. Nancy and a lot of the others would stay all night at Crane's, but Simon was motoring in. He had asked Nancy if he could take her back with him, but she had said: "Back to what? Aunt Edie?"

Aunt Edie was a great-aunt on Nancy's father's side. When Nancy was left high and dry on the shores of her parents' matrimonial differences, Aunt Edie came and played propriety. As she was over seventy and on a diet, her presence added little to the joy of Nancy's days.

Entering one of the big shops, Nancy made her way to the toy department. She had to buy something for Grace Marquis's twins. She could charge whatever she bought, and her sense of loneliness and depression dropped from her as she found herself in the midst of the crowds of children who, thrilled and excited, explored this modern fairyland.

She made her purchase and wandered to where the dolls were displayed in a section especially devoted to them. It was not the dolls which interested her as much as the faces of the little girls who were bunched in adoring groups about them. Here were the future mothers, drawn to these artificial babies by their potential maternity. With cheeks glowing, eyes shining, they hovered over the infants in bassinets, toddlers in rompers and short skirts, and the larger dolls grand as Cinderella at the famous ball.

One doll, lovelier than the rest, was enthroned on a pedestal. With blonde curls, blue eyes, and dimples, with rosy cheeks and a rosier frock, she was entrancing.

A little voice at Nancy's side said, "I want that one, Mother."

"I wish you might have it, Wendy, but we only came to look."

"Perhaps Santa Claus will bring it," the girl said hopefully.

"Oh, darling!" There was dismay in the mother's voice. "You mustn't be disappointed if he doesn't."

The little voice went on: "Well, maybe he will. He will know she would like me for a mother."

"I am sure she would, but—" The rest was lost in the babble of voices.

Turning a little, Nancy saw the mother and the child. Very shabby, the mother thin but smiling, the child enchanted by the peep into fairyland. Their presence in this great and fashionable place was undoubtedly an adventure into the unknown. The mother had brought her child to see, not to buy. Nancy liked the mother's voice. There was sweetness in it and a quality less tangible than sweetness. Courage, perhaps, or fortitude.

They were moving on.

"Do you think, Mother," the child was piping, "that Santa Claus might—?"

Nancy found herself following them. She had never bothered much about children. The sons and daughters of her friends were restless little creatures, a bit bored by life. Not like this child—hopeful, eager.

As they came out at last into the snowy street, the mother raised an umbrella. It was one of those with ribs poking through, but it sheltered the shabby pair from the snow, and the child hopped along by her mother's side like a happy robin.

With Nancy still following, they turned into a street which tapered off suddenly from elegance to squalor. Arriving at a grimy tenement, the mother and child ascended the steps and went in.

Nancy stood outside in the snow. She, too, carried an umbrella, but it was not one with ribs poking through. It was, indeed, particularly attractive, and Simon had given it to her. It had a jade ball on the handle, and the silk was a deeper shade. Nancy's hair was bright under her smart little hat, and the fur of her coat was as soft as a pussycat's. The coat had cost a fabulous sum. Nancy's father had given it to her because he was leaving her alone for Christmas while he cruised the Caribbean. Nancy felt that its richness was out of place in the squalor about her.

Looking up, she saw the child's face in the window on the second floor. Nancy waved, and the child waved back, and her eyes followed the lovely lady with interest.

Returning to the shop, Nancy bought the doll. She thought it better to deliver it herself than to send it. So back she went to the shabby street, her umbrella bobbing.

When she arrived at the grimy tenement, the child was not at the window. Nancy, ascending the stairs, set the box out of sight in the hall and knocked at a door on the second floor.

The mother of the child opened it.

Nancy said, "Could I speak to you a moment out here?"

The woman shut the door behind her, and Nancy found herself stammering: "I heard your little girl wish for the doll. I bought it. I want her to have it."

The woman faltered, "The doll in the shop?"

"Yes."

"Oh!" A flush came into the mother's cheeks. "A doll like that is too handsome for Wendy."

"But she wanted it."

"We want many things we can't have. Wendy needs other things." She stopped and forced a smile. "I'm afraid I must seem ungrateful. It is so good of you, but—" she stopped again.

There was a moment's awkward silence, then the woman said with a touch of wistfulness: "Perhaps I am wrong. Perhaps I should let her have it. Perhaps it will be worth while, if no other dreams come true for her, that this one will—" Her voice broke on that.

Nancy said impulsively, "Can't I help?"

The woman shook her head. "We're all right. And I'll let Wendy have the doll."

"I want her to think that Santa Claus brought it. It's such a darling thing to believe in Santa Claus and so dreadful when we don't."

"Yes," the woman said. "Santa Claus is kindness. I tell Wendy that, but she still clings to the idea of a saint with whiskers and sleigh bells. And if it makes her happier, why not?"

"Why not?" said Nancy, who didn't believe in anything.

The woman said, hesitating a little on the words: "Would you come in? I'd like to have you see my baby."

"I'd love to."

* * *

The room that they entered was very clean and bare. A well-scrubbed table was set with two plates and two cups. There was a basket of bread, a glass of milk for Wendy, and a little pot boiling on the stove gave out the savory odor of soup. Wendy, rising from her seat, was wide-eyed at the vision of loveliness in the pussycat coat.

Nancy held out her hands to her. "I'm Nancy Spaulding," she said, "and I've come to see the baby."

Wendy proudly led the way to where the baby lay. "His name," she said, "is Timothy."

"Timothy Bryan," the mother said. "I am Mrs. Bryan, and Wendy is Wendy Bryan."

With the introductions thus accomplished, the woman lifted the baby in her arms. Her eyes were happy as she looked at him. It seemed to Nancy incredible that with all the shabbiness, all the bareness of this poor home, the mother's eyes were happy.

She asked, "How old is he?"

"Six months. My husband died a year ago."

Nancy said, "Isn't it hard for you, having to take care of the two of them?"

"Hard? No. It's all that makes life worth living. I get sewing from one of the big shops, and I have milk for my babies and food enough for my strength. The hard thing was losing my husband. I loved him. But in my children he lives again. I think sometimes it is like the way I feel about our Lord at Christmas, that God lives in Him, in human form."

Tears were close to Nancy's eyes. She hadn't cried for years, not since that awful night when she had known that Daddy and Mother hated each other and that her home was wrecked. But here was something—something that she wanted. This woman was rich in love, and Nancy was poor.

When, a little later, Nancy went away, she told herself that in spite of the woman's brave words, the need of the little family was great. Well, she'd see that they had a Christmas dinner, and she would tuck into an envelope a snug sum of money. She would have to borrow the money from Simon, darling Simon who never failed her—and who, that very night, if the gods were good, would ask her to marry him.

But Simon, as it happened, had no idea of asking Nancy to marry him. He loved her deeply, but she wasn't the kind of wife he wanted. A man had to be cautious in these days. The Meriweathers in the past had not been cautious—they had gone neck or nothing to their romantic enterprises, had plighted their troths at various Gretna Greens, or more conventionally at the altar, and had lived happily ever after—or unhappily, as the case might be.

But there had been this difference. The Meriweathers of previous generations had not had before them the menace of the divorce court. The wives of those earlier Simons had said solemnly at the altar, "Till death do us part." But the girls of Simon's set declared frankly and without shame that if they didn't like the men they married, they wouldn't live with them.

Nancy herself had said, "Do you think, if I made a mistake, I'd be tied for life to any man?"

And that wasn't Simon's idea of marriage. He wanted permanence. He wanted a wife who would help him to keep the green plant of their affection in full flower. He felt that he could love Nancy forever, but he feared that his love might not be enough to change her from a teasing sprite to a constant and contented spouse.

When Simon presented his matrimonial theories to Nancy for discussion, she held them up to scorn, calling him Simon Legree and Simple Simon and, now and then, wickedly, Simon Pure. Having no inferiority complex and only a normal amount of vanity, Simon had smiled through it all. But of late she had gone beyond teasing, beyond argument. She was playing around with Crane Mawson, and Simon's idea of a woman who would play around with Crane was not his idea of what he wanted in a wife.

❄ ❄ ❄

He thought of these things as he stood uncertainly before a case in Tiffany's great shop trying to choose a gift for Nancy's Christmas. He had always given her a present and had found little difficulty in selecting it, but this year it was different. For the first time he was definitely placing her among the other women of his acquaintance. Hitherto she had been set apart in his mind as the woman he was going to marry. To the woman a man didn't intend to marry, in these modern days, one gave perfumes in crystal flasks, bits of jade set in dull gold, carved coral in silver bracelets, aquamarine earrings if her eyes matched them. Simon knew the litany of up-to-date feminine demands.

He drew the line only at jeweled lipsticks and cigarette holders. He had told Nancy on one occasion that he loved his love with an "N" because she was Neat and N-chanting, and Nancy had said,

"Well, I don't get lipstick on your hanky or cigarette ashes on your shirt front, but there are worse things, darling."

"What?"

"Getting on people's nerves."

"Do I? On yours?"

"On everybody's."

Well, if she meant people like Crane Mawson, Simon didn't care how much he got on their nerves. Crane's real name was Derwent, but he had a long figure and a long neck, and at school the somewhat ludicrous combination had incited his mates to call him "Crane." He was no longer ludicrous. He had gained pounds and muscle at college and prestige at football. His fresh coloring and his shock of fair curls were high notes in the good looks he had acquired. But the name still stuck.

Crane would, of course, give Nancy a present. But that was not Simon's worry. His worry was to choose one for her himself. He had thought of a Baxter print. Nancy was always hunting for a Josephine to match her

Baxter Napoleon. Nobody seemed to know whether Baxter had ever really done Josephine, but Nancy had not given up the hunt as hopeless. She had a desultory interest in collections. She acquired things because every one seemed to do it.

Simon, who did nothing because other people did it, collected objects that had to do with the art of fishing. He loved the out-of-doors, and, having traveled much, had brought home with him nets and creels and flies, ancient and modern, primitive and up to date. He spent much time in cataloguing his treasures, or, in right season, whipping the streams of the North or doing deep-sea fishing in warmer waters. He was, indeed, very much in earnest about it, and his preoccupation had given Nancy an opportunity to call him Simon the Fisherman.

"If you think you are teasing me," he had told her, "you are thinking wrong. Simon Peter was rather splendid."

Nancy's level gaze had studied him. "He was a fisher of men. And you are a fisher of women. They are all in love with you."

"All of them? Not you, Nancy?"

"Well, of course. I couldn't be."

"Why not?"

"I've known you too long and too well."

It sounded harsh, but it wasn't, for she had made a face at him to show she wasn't quite in earnest. She had a lovely little face, and her eyes were as wide and as candid as when she had stuck out her tongue the first time he had met her. And her red hair was as bright and beautiful as when he had pulled her long curls in return for her impishness.

❄ ❄ ❄

It was when she was five that he had first given her a Christmas present—a pink china box filled with pink Jordan almonds and tied with pink ribbon. She had adored it and had kissed him. She had kissed him on Christmas Day every year until four years ago. Then she had said: "I'm grown up. I'm not going to kiss any man now till I've promised to marry him."

It was old-fashioned, of course, but Simon liked it. He hoped she had not failed in her resolve, though at times he feared it. Crane had been rushing Nancy beyond anything. Perhaps he had already asked her to marry him. Perhaps she had said, "Yes." Perhaps he had kissed her. Simon didn't like to think about it.

He was hanging now over a tray of old brooches. There was one that he wanted for Nancy. It was not large and was of exquisitely painted porcelain set about with pearls. It was expensive, far beyond anything that Simon had expected to pay. But the head painted on it was the head of a Madonna, and the Madonna looked like Nancy. There was the same rich coloring of eyes and hair, and she wore a blue cloak about her shoulders. Nancy wore blue a lot, and Simon liked it.

But why should he buy a brooch like that? Nancy wasn't the Madonna type. Yet he had an almost uncanny feeling that if the Madonna of the brooch lifted those modestly lowered lashes, she would show the impish, teasing eyes of Nancy.

Yet he wanted her to have it, and the extravagance would not break him. He wondered what Crane

Mawson would give her. And as if the thought had brought him, he heard Crane's voice behind him.

"Only one day more to Christmas, Simon, and I've got a list as long as your arm. Ten cigarette holders for ten girls. Ten vanity cases, ditto. That settles the masses, as it were, but there's still the one girl. Look here, Simon, if you wanted to buy something for the Only Woman in your life, what would you get?"

Simon straightened up, and when Simon stood straight, his inches seemed to top those of Crane.

"What would I give her? I should give her precisely nothing."

Crane laughed derisively. "You wouldn't get far with most women."

"Perhaps not with what you call the masses, but I might get farther with the one I wanted."

"Don't fool yourself, Simon. They can all be bought."

Simon did not answer. Why argue with Crane, who had millions and who could buy anything? Perhaps he could buy Nancy. Simon didn't want to buy a woman. He hadn't Crane's millions, and he was glad of it. And anyhow, why should he worry when he didn't want to marry Nancy?

Crane was saying, "Come over here and look at this."

He led the way to a case wherein were displayed certain gorgeous jewels. Crane had chosen from among the others a curled feather of diamonds tipped with emeralds. It could be worn, he explained eagerly, in a half dozen ways. "On her shoulder. In her hair—"

Nancy's shoulder! Nancy's hair!

"I've half a mind to get it for her," Crane told him. "Nancy, I mean. Think she'd object?"

"You'll have to decide that. It's you who are giving it."

"I'll toss a nickel. . . . Heads she gets it, tails she doesn't."

He flipped the coin, and the head came up. He was pleased and showed it. "The fates are with me," he said, and gave the clerk the order.

Simon said, "See you tonight," suddenly, and got out.

❄ ❄ ❄

It was snowing, and with his hat pulled down and no umbrella, he made his way through the driving storm. Taxi men hailed him, but he would have none of them. He welcomed the pit-pat of soft flakes against his cheek. His mind whirled with the snow.

If Nancy married Crane, she would be unhappy. And he, Simon, might save her. By all the passion that was in him, he knew it. He knew that if tonight he took her in his arms and told her on a rushing tide of eloquence that she was his and nobody else should have her, he might win her.

But what then? What of this Nancy he would win? In the last analysis, what did she ask of life?

A good time? Money to spend? Freedom from care? She had told him a thousand times, "I want to dance through life, Simon."

But one couldn't dance through life. Simon knew that. He had lived through his mother's dreadful illness, had seen the pain that no drugs could ease. He had known his father's devotion. He had seen his mother cling and gain courage in the arms that loved her. He knew of those days of poverty when his mother was young and pretty and the dishonesty of his father's partner had brought failure in business. He knew the depth of tenderness with which the young couple had sustained each other. He had seen his tiny sister die and his mother's fortitude in the face of tragedy. The watchword of his home had been love. Not love that asks for things, but a sharing. If Nancy couldn't share, he couldn't make her happy. He couldn't make any woman happy who shirked life. She would lose his respect, his love. A man had to fight with his back to the wall in these days, and he needed a woman to buckle on his armor.

He went back to his office, worked late, and got home in time to dine with his father. Anticipating the late supper, he ate little.

His father queried, "Where's your appetite?"

"I'm saving up. Crane's having a late supper on the ice—sausages and scrambled eggs."

"Nancy going?"

"Yes, and dozens of others."

"Chaperones?"

"There aren't any such animals in these days. But Crane's parents will be somewhere about the house. It's a huge place, you know, and Crane has his own quarters. I'm glad the snow stopped. The wind will blow the ice clear."

❄ ❄ ❄

Later, as they had their coffee in the living room, Simon's father said: "Your mother would be very happy if she knew you were going to marry Nancy. She loved her as a child and was sorry for her. . . ."

"I'm not going to marry her."

"She's refused you?"

"I'm not going to ask her."

The older Simon Meriweather cleared his throat. "My dear boy, I thought it was settled."

"I thought so, too. But I can't do it."

"Can you tell me why?"

"Yes. I am not sure that if we married, things would last with her—permanent things, like you and Mother."

His father stared into the fire. His voice was husky when he spoke. "I never doubted your mother."

Simon's voice was eager. "That's what I mean. I've known Nancy for fifteen years, yet I feel that I don't know her. She was a lovely little girl. She's lovely now. But she makes light of things that I don't want made light of by my wife, by the—mother of my children . . ."

He stumbled over those last words, and his father said gently, "One never quite knows in the beginning."

"You knew with Mother."

"I loved her."

Simon's head went up. "You think I don't love Nancy?"

"I think, if you loved her, you might see beneath the surface."

Simon stood up, and there was a poignant note in his voice as he spoke: "Dad, they all think I'm a prig about such things, that I ask too much. Do you?"

And now his father stood beside him, his hand on his son's shoulder.

"No. In a way you are right. A woman must prove her worth before a man can marry her."

When Simon arrived at Crane's, Nancy and the others were on the ice. Nancy never looked more lovely than in her skating clothes. Tonight she wore white wool. There was no touch of color except the red of her hair and the red-gold of the scarf which blazed like a bright banner as she skated with Crane.

Simon spoke of the scarf when at last he had a chance at her. "It's a beautiful thing."

"Crane bought it in Switzerland when he was there for winter sports. He sent it to me last Christmas, but this is the first time I've worn it."

Simon said abruptly, "I'm not going to give you a Christmas present."

She was startled. "Why not?"

"Everybody gives you things."

They skated on for a few moments in silence. Then Nancy said, "Of course you don't mean it."

"But I do."

She flashed a glance at him. "Have a heart, darling. I want something, if it's only a stick of candy."

"You'll get plenty of gifts. You won't miss mine."

Her laugh was low and provocative. "Jealous?"

"No." He could not tell her that it was something deeper than jealousy.

Their arms were linked, her hands in his, as they swayed in rhythmic motion. Simon was aware that Nancy's fingers had tightened on his, that her cheek was against his coat, that her face was lifted toward him.

"Be nice to me, Simon." Again the provocative note.

Simon, held by that note, his heart answering it,

knew that in another moment, if he wasn't careful, Nancy would be in his arms. He would be saying the things it wasn't wise to be saying. He would be saying the things that would sweep them both away from reason. And marriage was a reasonable estate!

He said, therefore, with a lightness that hid the tumult in his heart, "If we don't get back in a hurry, we'll miss the eats."

The fingers that had tightened on his relaxed. She drew away from him. It was all he could do not to draw her back, but he did not.

✳ ✳ ✳

In heavy silence they returned to where the crowd was gathered about a great fire that lighted the night, and where competent servants from Crane's huge house on the hill were doing expert things with gridirons and frying pans.

Nancy sat close to the fire, which, shining on her, showed her hair a mass of molten metal, and suddenly she said: "Let's play Consequences. I'll begin. I love my love with an 'S' because he is Stingy."

All eyes were turned on Simon.

"She means you," said several accusing voices.

He was cool. "Does she? Well, I love my love with an 'N' because she's Nonsensical."

Nancy came back with, "I love my love with a 'C' because he's Charming." She smiled at Crane.

Crane was standing beside her, his plate in his hand. His skating clothes were as blue as his eyes, and with his height and yellow hair he was like some young god of the old Norse legends. His laugh was strong and hearty as he flung his challenge back, "I love my love with an 'N,' because she's—Necessary."

Nancy flushed. "You're so obvious, Crane. And anyhow it's a stupid game." She stood up. "If you're all going to keep on eating, I'll sing for you. It's a song Simon taught me years ago."

She saw Simon's startled face. She knew he would hate having her sing before all these people the song which each Christmas they had sung alone together. Not that they had been sentimental about it, but each had felt that the silly little song meant something that was not on the surface. Yes, Simon would hate having her sing it. Well, let him. All the old things between them were dead. He had killed them when he had said, "If we don't get back, we'll miss the eats."

Nothing could have been more revolting. That he could think of food when her head had been ready to tuck into the hollow of his shoulder, and when he had known, if he had any warmth in him, that she wanted him to take her in his arms. And he had not taken her. He had not wanted her.

She began to sing:

A ship, a ship a-sailing,
A-sailing on the sea,
And it was deeply laden
With pretty things for me.

There were raisins in the cabin
And almonds in the hold;

> *The sails were made of satin,*
> *And the mast it was of gold. . . .*

As the verse ended, there was a cry from the crowd: "Go on. Go on."

Nancy said, "Sing, everybody," and Crane joined in, and the others, stumbling over some of the words but getting the tune.

Simon was not singing. He sat staring at Nancy, and suddenly she stopped.

"Sing, Simon," she said.

He shook his head. "I've forgotten the words," he told her.

He saw her face grow white, but she finished the song bravely.

> *The captain was a duck, a duck,*
> *With a jacket on his back,*
> *And when the fairy ship set sail,*
> *The captain he said, "Quack."*

❄ ❄ ❄

An hour later, in Crane's big house, she was saying to Simon with sobbing breath: "I'll never forgive you, never. You lied to me. You couldn't have forgotten the words—"

"Yes," he said sternly, "I have forgotten everything but that I love you, and that you could sing our song before all those grinning people."

He had not intended to say it, but, having said it, he turned on his heel and left her. They had been standing

on the great stairway, and Nancy had peeled off her
jacket and sweater. In her silk shirt and wool breeches
she was like a handsome boy. And as she stood there
alone when Simon had gone, Crane's eyes were on her
Rosalind-like beauty.

He crossed the room. "Look here," he said, "I want
to show you something."

"I'm dead for sleep. Wait till tomorrow."

"I don't want to wait, and you won't when I show
you. Come on, darling."

She followed him upstairs to a small sitting room
where he unlocked a cabinet, took out a box, and
showed her, lying in a satin nest, the curled feather of
diamonds tipped with emeralds. "You can wear it," he
said, as he had said in the shop, "in a dozen ways. On
your shoulder. In your hair—"

He stopped, for she was looking at him with eyes that
were wide and stormy.

"You know I can't accept a thing like that from you,
Crane."

"Why not? There are no strings tied to it."

"Aren't there?"

"Well, of course. I'm simply mad about you, and I
want you for my wife. I can give you everything—"

She said sharply, "I'm not to be bought."

He laughed. "Simon said that this afternoon."

"Where?"

"In the shop. I showed him this. I tossed a nickel
to see whether I dared give it to you. I wasn't going to
give it to you tonight, but when you were singing that
song, you were like something out of a dream, and I
knew I could never be happy without you."

She did not answer. She was looking down at the glittering feather. Oh, she didn't want to be a part of any one's dream but Simon's. Simon, who couldn't give her things like this. Simon, who had flung her love back in her face and had left her.

Crane was leaning down to her. "Darling—"

She gave him a little push. "Please—" she said in a breathless way, and ran madly up the stairs.

She found her room, locked the door, and flung herself on the bed sobbing. She had lost Simon. Why or how, she couldn't quite decide. Perhaps it was that silly song. Perhaps it was because he had seen Crane's present and had thought she might be bought.

Well, whatever it was, her Christmas was spoiled. There remained only to give to Wendy and the mother of Wendy something of Christmas joy. She thought of the mother's eyes as she had looked at her baby. And the things she had said of her husband. That in the children he still lived for the woman who loved him. Oh, if love had only been like that for her own father and mother. If only it might be like that for herself and Simon!

She slept at last and went away the next morning before any one was up. She left a note for Crane: "I'm sorry, but I can't stay any longer. I think you will understand."

❄ ❄ ❄

Arriving home, she made out the market list for the Christmas basket to be sent to Mrs. Bryan. There must be a chicken for roasting, and all the things to go with it; a tree and toys for Wendy and the baby; a loaf of bread to be delivered every day until the order was canceled; milk, too, must be sent daily.

All these things could be charged to her father's account, and certain warm garments and toys for the children could also be charged. Bob Spaulding never complained of bills, especially those of his daughter. In a way he loved her, but he had not loved her enough to live his life sanely and decently.

Her lists finished, she went to the cook with them. The chicken was to be roasted at home, and there would be gravy and mashed potatoes and other vegetables, all sent hot tomorrow. The tree Nancy would take over this afternoon and trim, and on her way to the toy shop she stopped and arranged with Mrs. Bryan that Wendy could be sent to a neighbor's so that the decorating might be done secretly.

There would be, she told herself with a flame of resentment sweeping her, no money to tuck in with the other things. For she couldn't borrow of Simon, not after the things that had happened. There was, of course, Aunt Edie, but Aunt Edie didn't believe in borrowing or lending.

At the lunch table Aunt Edie demanded: "Why aren't you eating, Nancy? Girls of today starve themselves. I wonder that they think of themselves as future mothers."

Nancy did not answer. Her mind was not on food or on the future. She was thinking of Simon. By this time he was on his way to Vermont. In a few hours he would be dining with his grandmother, having those famous biscuits and maple syrup of which he had bragged. Men were like that. They would eat though the heavens fell!

But Simon was not on his way to Vermont. He was to leave town with his father at five-thirty. He was very busy, but all the morning, as he had worked over his papers, his mind had been distracted by thoughts of Nancy. He had a feeling that last night he had been brutal. But there was nothing to be done about it. He couldn't ask her to marry him. Not with his ideas of what marriage meant. And anyhow by this time she was probably engaged to Crane.

When the lunch hour arrived, he rushed to his club, had a glass of milk and not much with it, and was rushing out again when he met Crane Mawson. He would have rushed on, but Crane stopped him and said abruptly, "Well, I couldn't buy her. . . ."

Simon stared at him. "Nancy?"

"Yes. I've taken that diamond feather back to Tiffany's. She wouldn't have it. She left my house before breakfast, and she left me flat. How's that for a merry Christmas?"

Simon, trying to be casual, said, "Perhaps better luck will come with the New Year."

"Better luck? Don't you believe it! If you had bet a thousand dollars yesterday that money couldn't buy a woman, you would have won it."

But Simon wasn't thinking of a thousand dollars. He was thinking that he must get back to Tiffany's and buy that brooch for Nancy. Even if he didn't approve of her, even if she was selfish and shallow and all the things that, God help him, he had said about her, she was still the little girl to whom he had once given the pink Jordan almonds in the pink box and who had kissed him and thanked him. He must think of that little girl Nancy, and of the Nancy who wouldn't be bought by Crane's jewels. Perhaps he could think of the two as one. Perhaps if he had thought of her in that way always, he wouldn't have been so smug and self-satisfied.

He looked at his watch. Time enough to run around to Tiffany's. Hailing a taxi, he rushed to the shop, bought the brooch, and, arriving at Nancy's, found her out.

"Do you know where she is?" he asked Aunt Edie.

Aunt Edie said, with some asperity: "She never tells me. You might ask Graham."

Graham was the butler. Miss Nancy had, he believed, some poor family on her mind. He thought cook might have the address. Cook had it, having noted it for the bread man. Simon rushed on. In the taxi he thought of what he would say to Nancy. He wasn't going to ask her to marry him, but he was going to tell her he was sorry.

❄ ❄ ❄

And while he was thinking these things, Nancy, on her knees trimming the tree, said to Mrs. Bryan, "Do you think Wendy will like it?"

"She's never seen anything so pretty."

Nancy, sitting back on her heels, surveyed it—a thing of shining balls and silver snow, of tinsel. "It is rather nice. I'll finish it up and hide it in the closet while you go for Wendy."

The mother, pulling on her coat, said, "If you'll just keep an eye on the baby—"

But Nancy, tying balls and draping tinsel, did not think of the baby until a little cry roused her.

"Darling . . ." She went to the basket and bent above it.

The baby stopped crying and smiled at her. She said almost shyly, "Hello, little Timothy."

Timothy. What a nice name! A Bible name. She liked Bible names. There was Simon, for instance. Simon, the Fisherman. Simon Peter. Rather a solemn name for a baby. She lifted the baby suddenly and hugged him. He was so adorable and warm and soft.

"Little Timothy," she said softly. "Little Timothy."

A knock sounded, and as she called, "Come in," the door opened, and Simon stood on the threshold.

He spoke with a touch of awkwardness, "Well, here I am."

"How did you find me?"

"They told me at the house," he answered, yet hardly knew what he was saying. For in back of Nancy was a window, and the red-gold of the winter sunset lighted the blue of her dress and shone on her hair and on the head of the baby in her arms. *Oh, Madonna, Madonna,* were the words in Simon's heart; but he could not speak them.

She held up the baby for him to see. "He's sweet, isn't he?"

"You're sweet." His voice wavered.

Their eyes met, and the look in Simon's made Nancy say hastily, "You see, I wanted to do something for somebody's Christmas." She told him about the meeting with Wendy and her mother. "They'll be coming back in a few minutes, and we'd better hide the tree."

She laid the baby in his basket. "I'm glad you came, Simon. I want to borrow some money."

"How much?"

"Could you let me have fifty?"

"More if you want it."

He took out his wallet and was counting the bills when he was suddenly aware of an incredible sound. Nancy was crying. He crammed the wallet in his pocket and drew her around so that she was within the circle of his arm.

"Dear girl, what is it?"

"Oh," she said, "I thought I was never going to borrow of you again. And I wanted to help Mrs. Bryan. I can't tell you how I feel about her, Simon. She loved her husband, and he's dead. Yet he lives for her and the children. Death hasn't parted them. Yet life parted my father and my mother. If only they had felt that way about me—that they lived in me—I might have been different. It was love I needed, Simon, and I didn't have it."

He could not speak. He held her close. Oh, what a fool he had been not to know that the hurt heart of a child had found a strange satisfaction in hurting others!

He said at last, his voice hoarse with emotion: "You're mine, Nancy. You know it, and I know it. . . . And I want it to be forever."

"Not like Father and Mother?"

"Never like them, dearest."

They heard the voice of Wendy in the hall. When

she opened the door, the tree was hidden. She was much excited.

"Santa Claus *is* coming. Mother says so. Perhaps he will bring me a doll."

Nancy bent and kissed her. "Perhaps."

"Mother says Santa Claus is kindness."

"He's more than that, darling. He's love, and every-thing—"

❄ ❄ ❄

Simon at last got Nancy away.

"We're catching a five o'clock train," he told Mrs. Bryan, "and we'll have to make a run for it."

Whirling along in a taxi, he told Nancy, "We'll stop at the house for your bag."

"But, Simon—"

"You're going to Vermont with us. If my grand-mother is going to be yours, she might as well give you a Christmas dinner."

The early darkness had come, and Nancy's head was on his shoulder. As they passed a street corner, a man in cheap Santa Claus clothes stood where the light shone on him. There were other cheap Santas on other corners. Too many of them, perhaps, but could there be too many? Santa Claus, the child had said, was kindness, and he, Simon, had not been kind. Well, he had the whole future in which to make up for it. To teach Nancy the love she had missed. And he would teach her in all humility. He who had misjudged her.

He said, "I've a present for you."

Her laugh was low. "A stick of candy, Simon?"

"Something better than that."

But he could not tell her. Tomorrow early, on Christmas morning, he would give her the Madonna, and she would know all that it meant to him.

(Irene) Temple Bailey
(?–1953)

(Irene) Temple Bailey (?–1953) was born in Petersburg, Virginia, and became one of the most popular—and highest paid—authors in the world during the first three decades of the twentieth century. Besides writing hundreds of stories that were published by the leading family magazines of her day, she also wrote books, including *Judy* (1907), *The Trumpeter Swan* (1920), *The Holly Hedge* (1925), and *The Wild Wind* (1930).

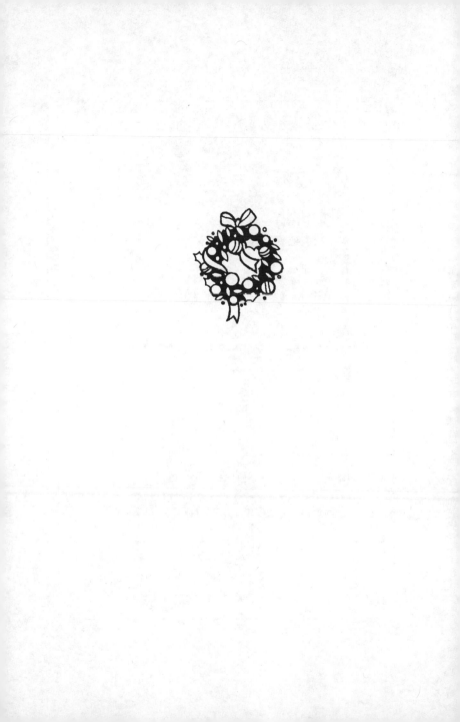

Joyce Reagin

OUR PART OF THE CIRCLE

For some people, a hundred dollars might not amount to much, but for this particular family, the loss was devastating! Its loss meant no Christmas. No Christmas after all those months of tight budgets and gradual saving. Worst of all, it was all in cash, in an envelope without any owner identification!

What to do?

*D*ecember 7, 1980, was one of those pre-Christmas Sundays that was meant to be full of candles, carols and great expectations. After church my husband, Earl, and I planned to take our young sons for a holiday portrait. Then a ride to look at neighborhood Christmas decorations would put us in the mood for a family shopping trip punctuated by whisperings and giggled secrets.

We missed church. On top of that, Grant, age seven, and his brother, Britt, age four, did *not* want to get dressed up for a photograph sitting. They whined all the way to the studio, where the photographer could find no evidence of our appointment and could not work us in. The ensuing Christmas ride was more dismal yet. But the capper was yet to come. We reached home only to discover that the rest of our Christmas money was gone. I had lost about a hundred dollars in cash.

A hundred dollars might not be a lot of money to lose, but it was important to us because we had, for the first time in our marriage, managed to adhere strictly to a Christmas budget.

Perhaps I'd been a little too proud! That very afternoon, while riding around in the car, I'd drawn the gray bank envelope from my purse and shown the bills inside to Earl and the boys. "Aren't you proud of me? Mom's actually managed to budget the Christmas money!"

That was the last time any of us saw the envelope. Evidently I had not put it back into my purse but had laid it on the seat. During the course of our afternoon stops, it must have fallen unnoticed from the car.

"It's Christmas," I explained to Earl. "People *steal* money this time of year. I'm sure someone has found it.

An envelope full of cash, with no name, no identification! Who could blame someone for keeping it?"

All evening I stewed. As we prepared for bed, Earl put his arms around me and kissed me. "Please, darling, stop thinking about the money. Tomorrow we'll retrace our steps. Who knows? Maybe someone has turned it in." We prayed together that I'd have peace about the money and that we'd find it again if it was God's will.

It didn't help a bit. I tossed and turned all night.

The next morning it was difficult to concentrate on teaching my classes at school. I kept thinking about the lost money, about my carelessness, my stupidity, about the gifts we still had to buy.

And then it came to me—the two hundred dollars.

Since early fall, Earl and I had set aside two hundred dollars in a savings account because we felt God wanted us to give that money to an individual or family in need. We'd been asking God to direct our path.

Then a stronger, inner voice reminded me, that was not our money, that was God's money. As tempting as it was, that money was not for me to spend.

After work, Earl and I retraced our path. No one had turned in money at the filling station where we'd bought gas. Nor had anything been found at the cemetery, where we'd taken flowers to my grandmother's grave. The driveway at our own home was empty, of course.

But a change was beginning to take place in me. At home that night, I went into the bedroom and knelt alone. "Dear God," I prayed, "I can't stand this worried feeling. Please help me to release this matter to You. I know that *all* of our money is Yours, including that hundred dollars. If it's Your will, please return the money to us. If it's not, I release that money. I give it freely to You and, through You, to whoever found it.

"And," I added, "I also release my carelessness on Sunday. If You can use even that for good, please go ahead. In Jesus' name, amen."

A peace stole over me. Not surprisingly, the house seemed brighter. The boys started laughing again, and we all joined in on snatches of carols.

The next day the sky was the brilliant blue that God saves for winter skies. I hummed as I headed for school, and taught my lessons without even thinking of the money.

Then, just before break time, I heard a still, small voice. *Go and call the places where you stopped on Sunday.*

But God, I thought, *we went back to all those places yesterday.*

Go and call.

Obediently, excitedly, I hurried to the phone. First I called the gas station. "I may have lost some money there," I began.

"No," the lady clipped.

Next was the cemetery. I felt funny about making that call, but I dialed anyway. The manager answered.

Feeling foolish, I said, "Last Sunday I lost some money—"

He interrupted me. "How much?"

"Almost a hundred dollars. The money was stuffed into a gray bank envelope."

"How about ninety-six dollars?" he asked.

"You have it!" I exclaimed.

"Sure do. A grave digger found it while he was picking up trash. He turned it in, said he thought it might be somebody's Christmas money."

After school I rushed to the cemetery office. The man who found it, Rubin Sales, was not there. Holding the dirt-smeared, tire-streaked envelope, I marveled that he had even bothered to look inside.

"Please tell him thank you," I said, leaving ten dollars for him.

I wasn't even out of the cemetery before that quiet voice spoke once more. *Rubin Sales is the one I want you to give the two hundred dollars to.* Excitedly I went to find Earl.

The very next day we went back to the cemetery to meet Rubin Sales. He was a middle-aged man, tall and muscular. But when we introduced ourselves, he looked at us almost shyly.

"Mr. Sales," I said, "thank you so much for finding and returning our money. Now we'd like to give some to you."

He firmly shook his head no without speaking.

"But, Mr. Sales—" I started.

"Thank you," he said, "but no. No reward. When I first saw that envelope, it just looked like trash. But something told me to look inside. Then something told me that was somebody's Christmas money." He paused. "I grew up poor. I know what it's like to hope and pray for something. And I didn't want any children's hopes not to come true."

"You don't understand," Earl answered. "This isn't a reward. This is God's money. We've been keeping it until He told us what to do with it. And we believe He's told us this two hundred dollars is yours."

No one spoke for a moment. Earl's odd pronounce-ment hung in the chilly air.

"Exactly two hundred dollars?" Sales asked. His voice had a strange crack to it.

We nodded.

"I've been scrimping and saving to meet my bills," he said, "and last night when I sat down to pay them, there wasn't even near enough. As I worried what to do, a program about world hunger came on the television. When I saw the faces of those starving children, my own problems seemed so tiny. I wanted to help so badly, but all I could do was pray. I prayed for a way to pay my bills so I could send the money I *had* saved to help those little ones."

"And how much are your bills?" Earl asked, although we already knew the answer.

"Exactly two hundred dollars," he said.

"Merry Christmas, Mr. Sales," I said as we handed him the envelope.

Joyce Reagin

Joyce Reagin of Greenwood, South Carolina, wrote for family and inspirational magazines during the last half of the twentieth century.

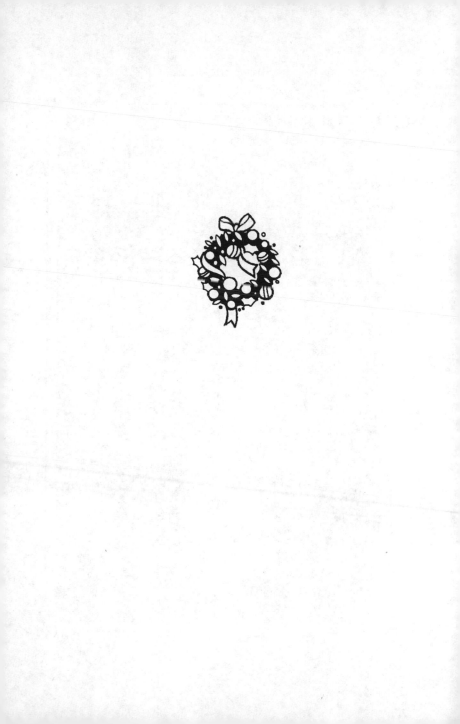

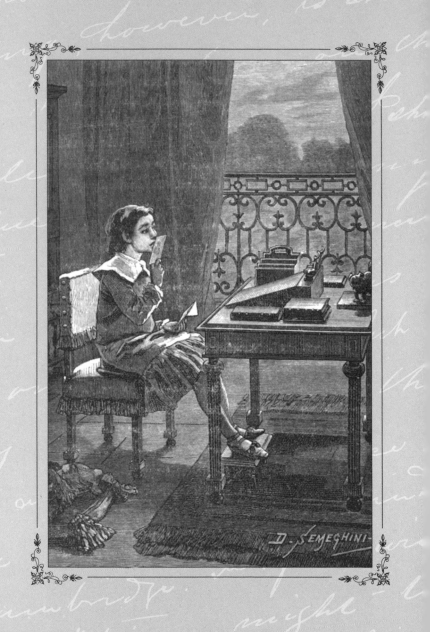

D. SEMEGHINI

THE FAMILY TWINKLE

Tamara was anything but happy. No Christmas in Christmassy Michigan this year—but instead a long flight and Christmas in Georgia with a grandmother she hardly remembered—and no Jeff, either.

But Grandma Lou didn't turn out to be . . . well, whatever she had feared she would be. Before the day was over, Tamara had learned a great deal about families—and even why Jesus was born into one.

*T*amara, are you planning to pout the entire time?" Mom said from the front seat. "Do I have to stop this car?"

My father's eyes twinkled at me in the rearview mirror. "Leave her alone, Maggie," he said quietly to my mother.

It was cool that my dad understood, but as I glared miserably at the Georgia pines whipping past me outside the rental car, I didn't feel much better. With each passing swamp that took us farther from Michigan—and Jeff—I became gloomier.

"I don't want you sulking around Grandma Lou," Mom couldn't resist saying. "This is her last Christmas in her own house before she moves into the retirement home, and we all want this to be a real celebration for our family."

"Does Tammy *have* to enjoy it?" my father teased.

"Yes!" Mom said.

I snorted silently. I wasn't planning on enjoying *anything* this Christmas that didn't involve Jeff and my friends. I'd had it with "family" talk on this trip already.

"Well," Mom said, just before Dad caught her in a one-armed headlock, "just be sure your father's grandmother doesn't know you're brooding."

"Better put a bag over your head, Tam," Dad said.

THE REUNION

I hadn't been to Waycross, Georgia, since I was six, and none of the white-columned houses and funky little grocery stores looked familiar. Even when we drove up to Grandma Lou's there was no nostalgia. I just wanted to be in Michigan putting on my ice skates—with Jeff.

What seemed like forty-seven children belched from the front door when we drove up.

"Is that Bill's little Heather?" my mother said. "Goodness, has she grown!"

How she could tell one kid from another was beyond me. I stood by the car as they danced around like banshees.

The grown-ups gathered on the porch as if Princess Di were about to appear. When Grandma Lou emerged through the screen door, I had to look twice. Ten years is a long time when a person is going from 75 to 85. This wizened lady with the thinning, snowy hair bore almost no resemblance to the woman who'd been riding horses and hurling hay bales the last time I was there. Reluctantly, I approached the porch to give my duty hug.

"Here's our Tamara," Dad said.

"*I* can see that," Grandma Lou scolded him. She surveyed me out of her pecan-brown face and said, "You'll be wanting your own room."

I was grateful for that, and the first thing I did was write a letter to Jeff. I told him I didn't know how I was going to be able to stand two weeks away from him and all the kids we hung out with.

I didn't want Mom to know I was already writing him, so I couldn't ask her for a stamp. Then a memory popped in. I'd helped Grandma Lou mail her bills once, and I'd been thrilled as a kid to find out that the stamps were in a secret compartment in her desk.

The rest of our enormous family was in the kitchen, presumably feasting on Grandma Lou's famous fruitcake that I was supposed to love. They were making too much noise to hear me slip into the library and close the door.

There was definitely a smell in the room; I remembered that, too. It was a combination of honeysuckle and old books and lemon furniture polish. The scent slowed me down for a minute. It was so definitely *her*.

But Jeff was what was important right then. I opened the front of the cherry desk, and as I moved several slim leather volumes aside, one fell open. The smell wafted from it as I looked closer at the perfect curlicues of writing on its pages.

"Today, I met a boy—" said the violet ink.

"Ah, so you've found my journals."

I jerked back my hand and let the book fall to the rug. Grandma Lou leaned over to pick it up.

"I've left these to you in my will," she said. "But you're going to have to wait until I die to read them. I'm not finished with them yet."

There was a familiar twinkle in her eye as she laid the journal carefully back in the desk.

I knew my face was the color of her poinsettias, and I groped for something—anything—to say.

"I didn't mean to . . . I was actually looking for a stamp—"

"Ah." Her fingers deftly pushed open the secret compartment. "Writing a love letter?" she said, handing me a 37-center.

"Well—yeah."

"I thought you had that look about you," she said. "Well, for heaven sakes, why don't you call him?"

"Long distance? From here?"

She twinkled at me again. "We've had phones here for several years."

"I didn't mean—"

"Call him," she said. Then she slipped out.

SHARING SECRETS

My fingers shook with excitement as I dialed Jeff's number, but I could have saved myself the trouble. The conversation went something like this:

"Jeff? Hi!"

"Tammy?"

"Yes! I'm calling from Georgia! Can you stand it? I miss—"

"Listen, Tam, can you call me back? We're just headin' out the door to go—Hey, Mike, knock it off—I'm comin'! Can you call me back?"

"I miss you."

"Yeah, me too—I'm comin', already! Gotta go, Tam."

I was shredding the letter when Grandma Lou appeared with a tea tray.

"He 'blew you off,' didn't he?" she said.

I exploded into surprised laughter.

"I watch television," Grandma Lou said. She twinkled her eyes softly. "God made boys to be slower growing up. He must've had His reasons—I don't know—but boys that age sure don't know how to be in love yet like we women want them to. Don't you fret."

Something about her made it *hard* to "fret." It was the twinkle, and I knew where I'd seen it before.

"I'd never noticed how much my dad looks like you," I said.

"And you look like him, so what does that tell you?" She chuckled. "Too bad God doesn't let you pick your relatives, huh?"

I nestled back with my tea into a brocade chair I now remembered dated back to the Civil War.

"What else do you know about boys?" I said.

She spent the rest of the afternoon telling me, while I laughed until tears splashed into my cup. Her eyes twinkled at me, and mine twinkled back.

After the third time a granddaughter-in-law peeked into the library, Grandma Lou stood up. "They think it's my nap time," she said.

I looked up at her shyly. "You've done so much for me this afternoon," I said. "Is there something I can do . . . I mean, to help?"

She didn't even have to think about it. "Yes! Keep your parents and the rest of my grown-up children and grandchildren out of my hair." She winked. "What's left of it, anyway!"

TRADITIONS

There was no snow on Christmas morning, but as I pulled back the lace curtain I decided I kind of liked the Georgia pines.

"Come on, Tammy!" said my little cousin Sarah—or Samantha—or Tabitha—one of them. "It's time to open presents!"

My mother would've been proud of me—I thought about Jeff only once and immediately discarded the idea that he would be freaking out over the romantic gift I'd left for him to open. The rest of the time, I was in stitches: little kids, mountains of wrapping paper, fruitcake nobody ate, the laughter of four generations. It was wonderful.

But the best part came when I found the package from Grandma Lou. Inside were several slim leather journals. One was blank.

"For writing about all the young men who will stumble clumsily through your life," she'd written on the inside. "God bless you . . . and them."

The others were filled with elegant violet writing and Grandma Lou's distinct fragrance.

"A piece of our family," she'd penned inside the first one. "Families are powerful. That's why Jesus was born into one."

I looked up to find her twinkling at me.

"I decided not to wait until I died," she said.

And I knew, in a way, she never really would. She was leaving her twinkle behind.

Nancy X. Rue

Nancy Rue of Lebanon, Tennessee, a novelist and short-story writer, is a frequent contributor to contemporary family and inspirational magazines. She is also author of the Christian Heritage historical fiction series published by Focus on the Family.

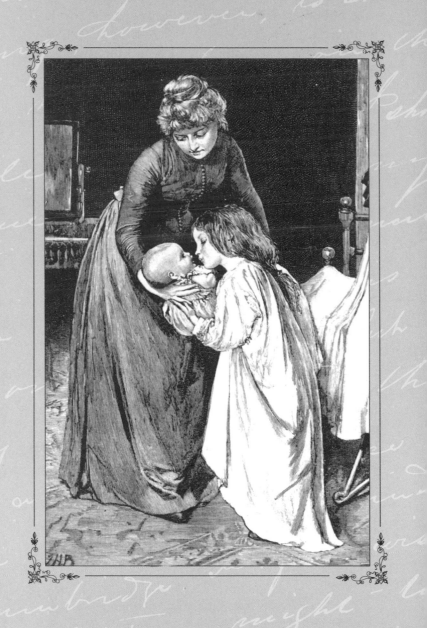

Kathleen Norris

CHRISTMAS BREAD

Doctor Madison was a very busy doctor—too busy to pay much attention to her little daughter, too busy to mend the broken relationship with her brother and his family.

But then came a scene in the attic, bread crusts in the pockets of an ancient-looking sweater, and a sudden change of mood.

This story is set right after World War I.

*B*ut what time will your operation be over, Mother?"

A silence. The surgeon opened three letters, looked at them, tore them in two, cast them aside, glanced at her newspaper, glanced at her coffee cup, and took a casual sip of the steaming liquid. But she did not answer.

"If you were thr-r-rough at 'leven o'clock—" Merle began again hopefully. She paid some attention to consonants, because until recently she had called *through* "froo," and she was anxious to seem grown-up. "I could go to the hospital with Miss Frothingham," she suggested, "and wait for you."

"I thought Miss Frothingham was going to take you to Mrs. Winchester's," Doctor Madison countered in surprise, at last giving partial attention to her little daughter. "Don't you want to spend Christmas Day with little Betty?" she went on, easily, half-absently. "It seems to me that is a very nice plan—straighten your shoulders, dear. It seems to me that it was extremely nice of Mrs. Winchester to want you to come. Most people want only their own families on Christmas Day!"

She was paying small heed to her own words. *That band really did straighten her teeth,* she was thinking. *I must remind Miss Frothingham to order some more of the little smocks; she doesn't look half so well in the blue-jacket blouses. How like George she is growing!* . . . "What did you say, Merle?" she added, realizing that the child's plaintive voice was lingering still in the air.

"I said that *I* would like my own family, too, on

Christmas," the child repeated, half-daring, half-uncertain.

"Ring the bell, dear," her mother said from the newspaper.

"I wish I didn't know what you were going to give me for Christmas, Mother!"

"You what?"

"I wish I didn't know what you were going to give me!"

Silence.

"For Christmas, you know?" Merle prompted. "I love your present. I love to have a little desk all my own. It's just like Betty's, too, only prettier. But I would drather have it a surprise, and run down Christmas morning to see what it was!"

"Don't say 'drather,' dear."

"Rather." With a gold spoon, Merle made a river through her cream of wheat in the monogrammed gold bowl and watched the cream rivers flood together. "What interests you in the paper, Mother?" she asked politely.

"Why, they are going to have the convention in California next summer," her mother said.

"And shall you go, Mother?"

"Oh, I think so! Perhaps you and Miss Frothingham will go with me."

"To hotels?"

"I suppose so."

Merle sighed. She did not like large strange hotels. "Mother, doesn't it seem funny to you that a patient would have his operation on Christmas Day? Couldn't he have it tomorrow, or wait till Wednesday?"

The doctor's fine mouth twitched at the corners. "Poor fellow, they can only get him here tomorrow, Merle, Christmas morning. And they tell me there is no time to lose."

Tears came into the little girl's eyes. "It doesn't seem—much—like Christmas," she murmured under her breath. "To have you in the surgery all morning, and me with the Winchesters, that aren't my relations at all—"

"Tell me exactly what you had planned to do, Merle," her mother suggested reasonably. "Perhaps we can manage it for some other day. What did you especially want to do?"

The kindly, logical tone was that of the surgeon used to matters no less vital than life and death. Merle raised her round, childish eyes to her mother's pleasant, keen ones. Then with a great sigh she returned to the golden bowl and spoon. Nothing more was said until Lizzy came in for the orders.

"Dear me, I miss Miss Frothingham!" said Doctor Madison then. "Tell Ada to use her own judgment, Lizzy. Tell her—you might have chicken again. That doesn't spoil, in case I'm late."

"You wouldn't have a turkey, Doctor? Tomorrow's Christmas, you know."

"Well—if Ada thinks so. I don't particularly care for turkey—yes, we may as well have a turkey. But no pudding, and above all, no mince pie, Lizzy. Have something simple—prune whip, applesauce, I don't care! Merle will be with the Winchesters all day, and she'll need only a light supper. If there are any telephones, I'm at the hospital. Miss Frothingham will be back this afternoon."

Then she was gone, and there was a long lonely day ahead of her small daughter. But Merle was accustomed to them. She went into the kitchen and watched Ada and Ada's friend, Mrs. Catawba Hercules, until Miss Watson came. Then she had a music lesson, and a French lesson, and after lunch she posted herself at a front window to watch the streets and wait for pretty Miss Frothingham, who filled the double post of secretary and governess, and who had gone home yesterday to her sister's house for a Christmas visit.

Outside was Christmas weather. All morning the streets had been bare and dark, and swept with menacing winds that hurried and buffeted the marketing and shopping women. But at noon the leaden sky had turned darker and darker, and crept lower and lower, and as Merle watched, the first timid snowflakes began to flutter whitely against the general grayness.

Then there was scurrying and laughter in the streets, bundles dampened, boys shouting and running, merry faces rouged by the pure, soft cold. The shabby, leather-sheathed doors of St. Martin's, opposite Merle's window, creaked and swung under the touch of wet, gloved hands. Merle could see the Christmas trees and the boxed oranges outside the State Street groceries coated with eider-down; naked gardens and fences and bare trees everywhere grew muffled and feathered and lovely. In the early twilight the whole happy town echoed with bells and horns and the clanking of snow-shovels.

By this time Miss Frothingham was back again, and was helping Merle into the picturesque black velvet with the deep lace collar. Merle, sputtering through the blue embroidered cloth while her face was being washed, asked how Miss Frothingham's little niece had liked her doll.

"Oh, my dear, she doesn't get it until she comes down-stairs tomorrow morning, of course!"

"Will she be excited?" Merle asked, excited herself.

"She'll be perfectly frantic! I see that your mother's present came."

"My desk. It came last night. I moved all my things into it today," Merle said. "It doesn't feel much like Christmas when a person gets their presents two days before," she observed.

"His presents. Her presents," corrected the governess.

"Her presents. Will your sister's little girls have a tree?"

"Oh, my, yes! It's a gorgeous tree!"

"And did you see my cousins while you were there?"

Miss Frothingham nodded. Her married sister lived next to Doctor Madison's brother, a struggling young engineer with a small family, in a certain not-too-fashionable suburb. There had been a difference of opinion, regarding a legacy, between the physician and her brother some years earlier, and a long silence had ensued, but Merle took a lively interest in the little cousins of whom she had only a hazy and wistful image, and her mother had no objection to an occasional mention of them.

"I saw Rawley—that's the second little boy—playing with my niece," Miss Frothingham said. "And I saw

Tommy—he's older than you—taking care of the baby.
I think he was going to the grocery for his mother; he
was wheeling the baby very carefully. But I think those
children are going to have a pretty sad Christmas
because their daddy is very sick, you know, and they all
had whooping-cough, and I think their mother is too
tired to know whether it's Christmas or Fourth of July!"

"Maybe their father's going to die like my father
did," Merle suggested stoically. "I guess they won't
hang up their stockings," she added suddenly.

For it had been reported that this was their custom,
and Merle liked to lie awake in her little bed, warm and
cosy on a winter night, and think thrillingly of what it
would be like to explore a bulging and lumpy stocking
of her own.

Miss Frothingham looked doubtful. "I don't suppose
they will!" she confirmed.

Merle was shocked. "Will they cry?"

"I don't suppose so. My sister says they're extremely
good children and will do anything to help their
mother."

"Maybe they'll hang them up anyway, and they'll be
empty?" Merle said, wide-eyed.

But the governess had lost interest in the subject, as
grown-ups so often and so maddeningly did, and was
manicuring her pretty nails, and humming, so Merle had
to abandon it for the moment.

However, she thought about it continually, and
after dinner she said suddenly and daringly to her
mother: "The Rutledge children's father is sick, and
they aren't going to hang up their stockings! Miss
Frothingham said so!"

When this was said, she and Miss Frothingham and her mother were all in the attic. Merle had not been there for weeks, nor her mother for months, and it was enchanting to the child to find herself bustling about so unexpectedly in this exciting atmosphere, which, if it was not typically Christmassy, was at least unusual. It had come about suddenly, as did much that affected her mother's movements.

The doctor had arrived home at half-past four, and Miss Frothingham had lost no time in reminding her that the promised bundle for the New Year's rummage sale for some charity was to have been ready this evening. Doctor Madison had said—did she remember?—that she had any amount of old clothing to dispose of.

"Oh, that attic is full of it!" Merle's mother had said, wearily. "You know this was my grandmother's house, and goodness only knows the rubbish that is up there! I've meant to get at it all some time—I couldn't do it in her lifetime. What time is it? Suppose we go up there and get a start?"

There was twilight in the attic, and outside the dormer windows the snow was falling. Merle performed a little pirouette of sheer ecstasy when they mounted the stairs. Her mother lighted the lights in a business-like fashion.

"Here, take this—take this—take this!" she began to say carelessly, picking one garment after another from the low row of ghostly forms dangling against the eaves. "Mr. Madison's army coats—"

"But, Mrs. Madison, this is beautiful beaver on this suit—yards of it!"

"Take it—take it!" Merle's mother said feverishly,

almost irritably. "Here, I shall never wear this fur coat again, and all these hats—I suppose those plumes are worth something!"

She was an energetic, restless creature. The hard work strangely calmed her, and just before dinner she was settling down to it almost with enjoyment. The summons to the meal annoyed her.

"Suppose we come back to it and make a thorough job?" she suggested.

Merle's heart leaped for joy.

"But you ought to be in bed, Kiddie," her mother said, not urgently, when dinner was over.

"Oh, Mother, please! It's Christmas Eve!" Merle begged, with all the force of her agonized eight years.

So here they all were again, and the snow was still falling outside, and the electric lights on their swinging cords were sending an eerie light over the miscellaneous shapes and contours of the attic, now making the shadow of an old what-not rush across the floor with startling vitality, now plunging the gloomy eaves behind Merle into alarming darkness.

Pyramids of books were on the floor, magazines tied in sixes with pink cord. Curtains, rugs, beds, heaped mattresses, trunks, the usual wheel-chair and the usual crutch—all the significant, gathered driftwood of sixty years of living was strewn and packed and heaped and hung about.

"Here, here's a wonderful patent preserving kettle,[2] do you suppose they could use that? And what about these four terrible patent rockers?"

"Oh, Mrs. Madison, I imagine they would be only

[2]A large open kettle used in one method of preserving fruits and vegetables

too delighted! Their idea is to open a regular store, you know, and make the sale permanent. But ought you—"

"I ought to have done it years before! But Doctor Madison—" His widow's breast rose on a sharp sigh; she lost the words for a second. "Doctor Madison and I never lived here, you know," she resumed. "And I stayed abroad for years after his death, when Merle was a baby. And for a long time I was like a person dazed—" She stopped.

"I had my work," she resumed, after a pause. "It saved my reason, I think. Perhaps—perhaps I went into it too hard. But I had to have—to do—something! My grand-parents died and left me this place and the Beachaways place, but I've had no time for housekeeping!"

"I should think not, indeed!" Miss Frothingham said, timidly respectful.

These fingers, that could cleave so neatly into the very stronghold of life, that could touch so boldly hearts that still pulsated and lungs that still were fanned by breath, were they to count silver spoons and quilt comforters?

The governess felt a little impressed; even a little touched. She did not often see her employer in this mood. Kind, just, reasonable, interested, capable, good, Doctor Madison always was. But this was something more.

"I had no intention of becoming rich, of being—successful!" the older woman added presently, in a dreamy tone. She was sitting with the great spread of a brocaded robe across her knee. Her eyes were absent.

"All the more fun!" Miss Frothingham said youthfully.

"I was alone—" Mary Madison said drearily and quietly, in a low tone, as if to herself. And in the three words the younger caught a glimpse of all the tragedy and loneliness of widowhood. "Doctor Madison was so wise," she began again. "I've always thought that if he had lived my life would have been different."

"You lost your parents, I know, and were you an only child?" Miss Frothingham ventured, after a respectful silence. But immediately the scarlet, apologetic color flooded her face, and she added hastily: "I beg your pardon! Of course I knew that you have a brother—I know Mr. Rutledge and his wife!"

"Yes, I have a brother," the doctor answered, rousing, and beginning briskly to sort and segregate again. The tone chilled her companion, and there was a pause.

"Your brother is Tommy's and Rawley's and the baby's father," Merle broke it by announcing flatly.

Her mother looked at her with an indulgent half-smile. She usually regarded Merle much as an amused stranger might have done; the odd little black-eyed, black-maned child who was always curling herself into corners about the house. *Merle is going to be pretty,* her mother thought tonight, in satisfaction. Her little face was blazing, her eyes shone, and she had pulled over her disheveled curls a fantastic tissue-paper cap of autumn leaves left from some long-ago Halloween frolic her mother could only half-remember.

"What do you know about them?" she asked good-naturedly. "You never saw them!"

"You told me once about them, when I was a teeny

little girl," Merle reminded her. "When we were in the cemetery you did. And Miss Frothingham told me."

"So there's a third child?" Doctor Madison asked, musing. Miss Frothingham nodded.

"A gorgeous boy. The handsomest baby I ever saw! . . . John," she said.

"John was my father's name. Sad, isn't it?" Doctor Madison asked after a silence during which she had folded the brocade and added it to the heap.

"A costumier would buy lots of this just as it stands," Miss Frothingham murmured by way of answer.

"I mean when families quarrel," persisted the doctor.

"Oh, I think it is very sad!" the secretary said fervently.

"We were inseparable, as children," Mary Madison said suddenly. "Tim is just a year younger than I."

"You're not going to give away all these beautiful Indian things, Doctor?"

The doctor, who had been staring absently into the shadows of the attic, roused herself. "Oh, why not? Merle here isn't the sort that will want to hoard them! I loathe them all. It was just this sort of rubbish—"

She had risen to fling open the top of one more trunk. Now she moved restlessly across the attic, and Merle, who did not know her mother in this mood, hopped after her.

"It was just this sort of rubbish, little girl," Mary Madison said gently, one of her thin, clever hands laid against the child's cheek, "that made trouble between— your Uncle Timothy and me. Just pictures and rugs—

and Aunt Lizzie's will. . . . Well, let's get through here, and away from these ghosts!"

"I wish *we* had three children," Merle said longingly. "You had your brother. But I haven't anyone! Did you hang up your stockings?"

"Dear me, yes! At the dining-room mantel."

"Then I would hang mine there, if I—hanged—it," Merle decided.

"But we have the big open fireplace in the sitting-room now, dear. We didn't have that when we were little, Timmy and I."

"But I'd drather in the dining-room, Mother, if that's what you did!"

"Here are perfectly good new flannels—" Miss Frothingham interposed.

"Take them. But Merle," the doctor said, a little troubled, "I would have filled a stocking for you if I had known you really wanted me to, dear. Will you remind me, next Christmas, and I'll see to it?"

"Yes, Mother," Merle promised, suddenly lifeless and subdued. "But next Christmas is so—so far," she faltered, with watering eyes and a trembling lip.

"But all the shops are closed now, dear," her mother reminded her sensibly. "You know, my brother and I never had a quarrel before," she added, after a long silence, to the younger woman. "And this was never an open breach."

"Was?" Miss Frothingham echoed, anxious and eager.

"Wasn't. No," said her employer thoughtfully. "It was just a misunderstanding—the wrong word said here, and the wrong construction put upon it there, and then resentment—and silence—our lives separated—"

She fell silent herself, but it was Merle, attentively watching her, who said now, "Their father's sick, and they aren't going to hang up their stockings!"

"Oh, they've had a great deal of trouble," Miss Frothingham added with a grave expression, as the older woman turned inquiring eyes upon her. "Mr. Rutledge has been ill for weeks, and the baby is quite small—six or seven months old, I suppose."

"Why, he's a successful man!" his sister said impatiently as the other paused.

"Oh, yes, they have a good Swedish maid, I know, and a little car, and all that! But I imagine this has been a terribly hard winter for them. They're lovely people, Doctor Madison," added little Miss Frothingham bravely and earnestly. "So wonderful with their children, and they had a little vegetable garden, and fruit trees, and all that! But all the children in that neighborhood had whooping-cough last fall, and I know Mr. Rutledge was pretty tired, and then he got double pneumonia before Thanksgiving, and he hasn't been out of the house since."

"He's a wonderful boy!" Doctor Madison said into a silence. "We were orphans, and he was a wonderful little brother to me. My grandparents were the stern, old-fashioned sort, but Timmy could put fun and life into punishment, even. Many an hour I've spent up here in this very attic with him—in disgrace."

She got up, walked a few paces across the bare floor, picked an old fur buggy-robe from a chair, looked at it absently, and put it down again.

"What insanity brought me up to this attic on a snowy Christmas Eve!" she demanded abruptly, laugh-

ing, but with the tears Miss Frothingham had never seen
there before in her eyes. "It all comes over me so—
what life was when Timmy and George—Merle's
father—were in it! Poor little girl," she added, sitting
down on a trunk and drawing Merle toward her; "you
were to have seven brothers and sisters, and a big daddy
to adore you and spoil you! And he had been two
months in his grave when she was born," she added to
the other woman.

"But then couldn't you afford to have all my brothers
and sisters?" Merle demanded anxiously.

"It couldn't be managed, dear. Life gets unmanage-
able, sometimes," her mother answered, smiling a little
sadly. "But a brother is a wonderful thing for a small
girl to have. Everything has robbed this child," she
added, "the silence between her uncle and me—her
father's death—my profession. If I had been merely a
general practitioner, as I was for three years," she went
on, "there would have been a score of what we call
'G.P.s' to fill her poor little stockings! But half *my*
grateful patients hardly know me by sight, much less
that I have a greedy little girl who has a stocking to be
filled!"

"Mother, I love you," Merle said, for the first time in
her life stirred by the unusual hour and mood, and by
the tender, half-sorrowful, and all-loving voice she had
never heard before.

"And I love you, little girl, even if I am too busy to
show it!" her mother answered seriously. "But here! Do
let's get done with this before we break our hearts!" she
added briskly, in a sudden change of mood. And she
sank upon her knees before a trunk and began vigor-

ously to deal with its contents. "And I'll tell you what I'll do, Merle," her mother went on, briskly lifting out and inspecting garments of all sorts. "I'll go and see Mr. Waldteufel on Wednesday—"

"Not Waldteufel of the Bazaar, Mother?"

"The very same. You know your daddy and I were boarding with his mother in Potsdam when the war broke out, and two years ago your mother saved his wife and his tiny baby—after two dear little babies had died. So he thinks a great deal of the Madisons, my dear, and he'll give me the very nicest things in that big shop for my little girl's stocking. And suppose you hang it up New Year's Eve this year, and next year—well, we won't say anything about next year now, but just you *wait!*"

"Oh, Mother—Mother!" Merle sang, her slippered feet dancing. And there was no question at this minute that she would some day be beautiful.

"Don't strangle me. There, I remember that dress— look at the puffed sleeves, Merle," said her mother, still exploring the trunk. "I suppose the velvet is worth something—and the lace collar. That was my best dress."

"Mother, mayn't I keep it? And wear it some day?"

"Why, I suppose you may. I wish," said the doctor in an undertone, whimsically to the other woman, "I wish I had more of that sort of sentiment—of tenderness—in me! I did have, once."

"Perhaps it was the sorrow—and then your taking your profession so hard?" Miss Frothingham suggested timidly.

"Perhaps—Here, this was my brother Timmy's

sweater," said the doctor, taking a bulky little garment of gray wool from the trunk. "How proud he was of it! It was his first—'my roll-top sweater,' he used to call it. I remember these two pockets—"

She ran her fingers——the beautifully tempered fingers of the surgeon—into one of the pockets as she spoke, and Merle and the secretary saw an odd expression come into her face. But when she withdrew her hand and exposed to them the palm, it was filled with nothing more comprehensible than eight or ten curled and crisped old crusts of bread.

"Mother, what is it?" Merle questioned, peering.

"Bait?" Miss Frothingham asked, smiling.

"Crusts," the older woman said in an odd voice.

"Crusts?" echoed the other two, utterly at a loss.

There was that in the doctor's look that made the moment significant.

"Yes," said Merle's mother. And for a full minute there was silence in the attic, Miss Frothingham covertly and somewhat bewilderedly studying her employer's face, Merle looking from one to the other with round eyes like those of a brunette doll. The older woman was staring into space, as if entirely unconscious of their presence.

The lights stirred, and shadows leaped and moved in answer. Snow made a delicate, tinkling sound outside, in the dark, on the roof beyond the dormers. The bell of Saint Paul's rang nine o'clock on Christmas Eve.

"I was always a stubborn child, and I hated the crusts of my bread, but they insisted that I eat them," said Mary Madison suddenly, in an odd, rather low voice.

"I used to cry and fight about it, and—and Timmy used to eat them for me."

"Did he like them, Mother?" Merle demanded, highly interested.

"Did he—? No, I don't know that he did. But he was a very good little brother to me, Merle. And Grandmother and Aunt Lizzie used to be stern with me, always trapping me into trouble, getting me into scenes where I screamed at them and they at me."

Her voice stopped, and for a second she was silent.

"Crusts were a great source of trouble," she resumed after a while.

"I like them!" Merle said encouragingly, to feed the conversation.

"Yours is a very different world, Baby. People used to excite and bewilder children thirty years ago. I've spent whole mornings sobbing and defiant. 'You will say it!' 'I won't say it'—hour after hour after hour."

Merle was actually pale at the thought.

"Timmy was the favorite, and how generous he was to me!" his sister said, musing. And suddenly she raised the little dried crusts in both hands to her face, and laid her cheek against them. "Oh, Timmy—Timmy—Timmy!" she said, between a laugh and a sob. "To think of the grimy little hand that put these here just because Molly—that's what Timmy always called me—was so naughty and so stubborn!

"Miss Frothingham," said Doctor Madison quietly, looking up with one of those amazing changes of mood that were the eternal bewilderment of those who dealt with her, "I wonder if you could finish this up? Get Lizzy to help you if you like; we're all but done any-

way! Use your own judgment, but when in doubt—
destroy! I believe—it's only nine o'clock! I believe I'll
go and see my brother! Come, Merle, get your coat
with the squirrel collar—it's cold!"

So then it was all Christmas magic, and just what
Christmas Eve should be. Saunders brought the little
closed car to the door, to be sure, but there he vanished
from the scene, and it was only Mother and Merle.

The streets were snowy, and snow frosted the windshield, and lights and people and the bright windows of
shops were all mixed up together, in a pink and blue
and gold dazzle of color.

But all this was past before they came to the "almost
country," as Merle called it, and there were gardens and
trees about the little houses, where lights streamed out
with an infinitely heartening and pleasant effect.

They stopped. "Put your arms tight about my neck,
Baby. I can't have you walking in this!" said her mother
then.

And Merle tightened her little furry arms about her
mother's furry collar, and they somehow struggled and
stumbled up to Uncle Tim's porch. There was light in
one of the windows, but no light in the hall. But after a
while footsteps came—

"Molly!" said the pale, tall, gentle woman who
opened the door, "and your dear baby!"

"Cassie—may we come in?" Merle had never heard
her mother speak in quite this tone before.

They went in to a sort of red-tinted dimness. But in
the dining-room there was sudden light, and they all
blinked at each other. And Merle instantly saw that over

the mantel two short stockings and tiny socks were suspended.

The women were talking in short sentences.

"Molly!"

"Cassie—"

"But in all this snow—"

"We didn't mind it."

"I'm so glad."

"Cassie—how thin you are, child! And you look so tired!"

"Timmy's been so ill!"

"But he's better?"

"Oh, yes—but so weak still!"

"You've had a nurse?"

"Not these last two weeks. We couldn't—we didn't—really need her. I have my wonderful Sigma in the kitchen, you know."

"But, my dear, with a tiny baby!"

The worn face brightened. "Ah, he's such a dear! I don't know what we would have done without him!"

A silence. Then Mrs. Rutledge said: "The worst is over, we hope. And the boys have been such a comfort!"

"They hung up their stockings," Merle commented in her deep, serious little voice.

"Yes, dear," their mother said eagerly, as if she were glad to have the little pause bridged. "But I'm afraid Santa Claus is going to be too busy to remember them this year! I've just been telling them that perhaps he wouldn't have time to put anything but some candy and some fruit in, this year!"

"*They* believe in Santa Claus," Merle remarked,

faintly reproachful, to her mother. "But I'm younger than Tommy, and I don't!"

"But you may if you want to, dear!" Doctor Madison said, shaken, yet laughing, and kneeling down to put her arms about the little girl. "Cassie, what can I do for Tim?" she pleaded. "We're neither of us children. I don't have to say that I'm sorry—that it's all been a bad dream of coldness and stupidity."

"Oh, Molly—Molly!" the other woman faltered. And tears came into the eyes that had not known them for hard and weary weeks. "He was to blame more than you—I always said so. He knew it! And he did try to write you! He's grieved over it so. But when he met you in the street that day—"

"I know it! I know it! He was wrong—I was wrong—you were the only sensible one, the peace-maker, between us!" the doctor said eagerly and quickly. "It's over. It's for us now to see that the children are wiser in their day and generation!"

"Ah, Molly, but you were always so wonderful!" faltered Cassie Rutledge. And suddenly the two women were in each other's arms. "Molly, we've missed—just *you*—so!" she sobbed.

Two small shabby boys in pajamas had come solemnly in from the direction of the kitchen, whence also proceeded the fretting of a baby. Merle was introduced to Tommy and Rawley and was shy. But she immediately took full charge of the baby.

"Santa Claus may not give us anything but apples and stuff," Rawley, who was six, confided. "Because Dad was sick, and there are lots of poor children this year!"

"And we aren't going to have any turkey because

Dad and John couldn't have any, anyway!" Tommy added philosophically.

John was the baby, who now looked dewily and sleepily at the company from above the teething biscuit with which he was smearing his entire countenance.

"He's getting a great, big, hard back tooth, Molly, at eight months," said his mother, casting aside the biscuit and wiping the exquisite, little velvet face. "Isn't that early?"

"It seems so to me. I forget! Any fever?"

"Oh, no, but his blessed little mouth is so hot! Timmy's asleep," said Cassie anxiously. "But Molly, if you could stay to see him just a minute when he wakes! Could Merle—we have an extra bed in the little room right off the boys' room, where the nurse slept. She couldn't spend Christmas with the boys? That would be better than any present to us!"

She spoke as one hardly hoping, and Merle felt no hope whatever. But to the amazement of both, the handsome, resolute face softened, and the doctor merely said: "Trot along to bed then, Merle, with your cousins. But mind you don't make any noise. Remember Uncle Timmy is ill!"

Merle strangled her with a kiss. There was a murmur of children's happy voices on the stairs. A messenger came back to ask if Tom's nine-year-old pajamas or Rawley's six-year-old size would best suit the guest. Another messenger came discreetly down and hung a fourth stocking at the dining-room mantel, with the air of one both invisible and inaudible.

"He's terrified," said Cassie in an aside, with her good

motherly smile; "he knows he has no business down-
stairs at this hour!"

Then Cassie's baby fretted himself off in her arms,
and the two women sat in the dim light, and talked and
talked and talked.

"Cassie, we've an enormous turkey—I'll send it over
the first thing in the morning."

"But, Molly, when Tim knows you've been here,
he'll not care about any turkey!"

"Their stockings—" mused the doctor, unhearing.

With a suddenly lighting face, after deep thought, she
went to the telephone in the dining-room, and three
minutes later a good husband and father, a mile away
across the city, left his own child and the tree he was
trimming and went to answer her summons.

"Mr. Waldteufel? This is Doctor Madison."

"Oh, Doctor!" came rushing the rich European
voice, "Merry Christmas to you! I wish could you but
zee your bapey—so fat we don't weigh him Sundays no
more! His lecks is like—"

The surgeon's voice interrupted. There was excited
interchange of words. Then the toy-king said: "I meet
you at my store in ten minutes! It is one more kindness
that you ask me to do it! My employees go home at
five—the boss he works late, isn't it? I should work hard
for this boy of mine—an egg he eats today, the big
rough-neck feller!"

❆ ❆ ❆

"Oh, Molly, you can't!" Cassie protested. But there was
color in her face.

"Oh, Cassie, I can! Have we a tree?"

"I couldn't. It wasn't the money, Molly—don't think that. But it was just being so tired . . . the trimmings are all there from last year . . . oh, Molly, into this darkness and cold again! You shouldn't!"

She was gone. But the hour that Cassie waited, dreaming, with the baby in her lap, was a restful hour, and when it was ended, and Molly was back again, the baby had to be carried upstairs, up to his crib, for there was heavy work to do below stairs.

Molly had a coaster and an enormous rocking-horse. She had the car loaded and strapped and covered with packages. She had a tree, which she said she had stolen from the grocer; he would be duly enlightened and paid tomorrow.

She flung off her heavy coat, pinned back her heavy hair, and tied on an apron. She snapped strings, scribbled cards. And she personally stuffed the three larger stockings.

Cassie assisted. Neither woman heard the clock strike ten, strike eleven.

"You'll be a wreck tomorrow, my dear!"

"Oh, Molly, no! This is just doing me a world of good. I had been feeling so depressed and so worried. But I believe—I do believe—that the worst of it is over now!"

"Which one gets this modeling clay? It's frightfully smelly stuff, but they all adore it! My dear, does Timmy usually sleep this way? I've looked in at him twice, he seems troubled—restless—"

"Yes—the scissors are there, right under your foot. Yes, he is like that, Molly, no real rest, and he doesn't seem to have any particular life in him. He seems so languid. Nothing tastes exactly right to him and of course the children are noisy, and the house is small. I want him—"

Mrs. Rutledge, working away busily in the litter, and fastening a large tinsel ball to a fragrant bough with thin, work-worn hands, stepped back, squinted critically, and turned to the next task. The homely little room was fire-warmed. Mary Madison remembered some of the books, and the big lamp, and the arm-chair that had belonged to her father. Cassie had a sort of gift for home-making, even in a perfectly commonplace eight-room suburban house, she mused.

"I want him," Cassie resumed presently, "to take us all down south somewhere—or to go by himself, for that matter!—and get a good rest. But he feels it isn't fair to Jim Prescott—his partner, you know. Only—" reasoned the wife, threading glassy little colored balls with wire, "only Tim is the real brains of the business, and Jim Prescott knows it. Timmy does all the design ing, and this year they've seemed to get their first real start—more orders than they can fill, really. And it worries Timmy to fall down just now! He wants to get back. But I feel that if he had a real rest "

"I don't know," the physician answered, setting John's big brown bear in an attitude of attack above the absurd little sock. "It's a very common attitude, and nine times out of ten a man is happier in his work than idling. I'd let him go back, if I were you, I think."

"Oh, would you, Molly?" Cassie demanded in relief and surprise.

"I think so. And then perhaps you could all get away early to Beachaways—"

"Molly!"

"Don't use that tone, my dear. The place wasn't even opened last year. I went to Canada for some hospital work, and took Merle with me and left her at the Lakes with my secretary. I wanted then to suggest that you and Timmy use Beachaways. It's in a bad condition, I know—"

"Bad condition! Right there on the beach, and all to ourselves! And he can get away every Friday night!"

"Perhaps you'll have my monkey down with her cousins, now and then. She doesn't seem to have made strangers of them, exactly."

"Not exactly," agreed Cassie with her quiet smile. "They were all crowded into the boys' big bed when I went up. I carried Rawley into the next room. Tom and Merle had their hands clasped, even in their sleep." She added suddenly, in an odd tone, "Molly, what—I have to ask you!—what made you come?"

"Christmas, perhaps," the doctor answered gravely, after a moment. "I've always wanted to. But, I'm kind of strange. I just couldn't."

"Tim's always wanted to," his wife said. "He's always said: 'There's no real reason for it! But life has just separated us, and we'll have to wait until it all comes straight naturally again.' "

"I don't think those things ever come straight naturally," said Mary Madison thoughtfully. "One thinks, 'Well, what's the difference? People aren't necessarily closer, or more congenial, just because they happen to be related!' But at Christmas time you find it's all true;

that families do belong together; that blood is thicker than water!"

"Or when you're in trouble, Molly, or in joy," the other woman said, musing. "Over and over again I've thought that I must go to you—must try to clear up the whole silly business! But you are away so much, and so bus—and so famous now—that somehow I always hesitated! And just lately, when it seemed—" her voice thickened, "when it seemed as if Timmy really might die," she went on with a little difficulty, "I've felt so much to blame! He's always loved you so, admired you—his big sister! He is always quoting you, what Molly says and does. And just to have the stupid years go on and on, and this silence between us, seemed so—so wasted!"

"Die!" Molly echoed scornfully. "Why should he? With these lovely boys and you to live for!"

"Yes, I know. But don't you remember saying years ago, when you were just beginning to study medicine in order to have an intelligent interest in George's work—don't you remember saying then that dying is a point of view? That you had seen a sudden sort of meekness come over persons who really weren't very sick, just as if they thought to themselves, *'What now? Oh, yes, I'm to die'*? I remember all our shouting when you said it, but many a time since, I've thought it was true. And somehow it's been almost that way with Timmy, lately. Just—dying, because he was through—living!"

"Cassie, what utter foolishness to talk that way, and get yourself crying when you are tired out, anyway!"

"Ah, well, I believe just the sight of you when he

wakes up is going to cure him, Molly!" his wife smiled through her tears.

But only a little later, the invalid fell, as it chanced, into the most restful sleep he had known for weeks, and Mary, creeping away to her car, under the cold, high moon, and hearing the Christmas bells ring midnight as she went over the muffling snow toward her own room and her own bed, could only promise that when she had had a bath, and some sleep, she would come back and perhaps be beside him when he awakened.

And so it happened that in the late dawn, when three little wrappered forms were stirring in the Rutledge nursery, and when thrilled whispers were sounding in the halls, Merle Madison was amazed to see her mother coming quietly up from the kitchen and could give her an ecstatic Christmas kiss.

"We know it's only oranges and candy," breathed Merle, "but we're going down to get our stockings now!"

"Is the tree lighted?" Mary Madison, who was carrying a steaming bowl, asked in French.

"It is simply a vision!" the other mother, whose pale face was radiant, answered, with her lips close to the curly head of the excited baby she was carrying. "Timmy's waking," she added, with a nod toward the bedroom door.

"I'll go in."

Molly carried her burden across the threshold—and in the quiet orderly sick room her eyes and her brother's eyes met for the first time in years.

He was very white and thin, unshorn, and somehow

he reminded her of the unkempt little motherless boy of
years ago.

"Molly!" he whispered, his lips trembling.

And her own mouth shook as she put the bowl on
the bedside table, and sat down beside him, and clasped
her fine, strong, warm hand over his thin one.

"Hello, Timmy," she said gently, blinking, and with a
little thickness of speech.

"Molly," he whispered again in infinite content. And
she felt his fingers tighten, and saw two tears slip
through the closed eyelids as his head was laid back
against the pillow.

"Weak—" he murmured, without stirring.

"You've been so sick, dear."

A silence. Then he said, "Molly, were you here in
the night?"

"Just to peep at you, Timmy."

"I thought you were. It was so delicious even to
dream it. I didn't dare ask Cassie, for fear it was only a
dream. Cassie's been an angel, Molly!"

"She always was, Tim. You and I were the demon
liars."

"'Demon liars!' Oh, do you remember the whipping
we got for yelling that at each other?"

"Do you remember that we agreed that 'yellow cats'
would mean all the very worst and naughtiest things that
ever were, and the grown-ups would never know what
it meant?"

He submitted childishly to her ministrations. She
washed his face, brushed his hair, settled herself beside
him with the steaming bowl.

"Come now, Timmy, Christmas breakfast!"

"Do you remember crying for Mother that first Christmas?"

"Ah, my dear! Imagine what she must have felt, to leave us!"

"I've thought of that so often, since the boys have grown big enough to love us, and want to be with us!"

"My girl is with them downstairs—I'll have to tell you what a Christmas we've made for them! The place looks like a toy-shop! Timmy, I hope they'll always like her, be to her like the brothers that she never had!" So much Mary said aloud. But to herself she was saying: *He doesn't seem to know it, but that's fully two ounces—three ounces—of good hot bread and milk he's taken.* "Well, was it a riot?" she added to Cassie, who came quietly in to sit on the foot of the bed and study the invalid with loving and anxious smiling eyes.

"Mary, you should have seen it! It was too wonderful," said Cassie, who had been crying. "I never saw anything like the expression on their little faces when I opened the door. Merle was absolutely white—Tom gave one yell! It was a sight—the candles all lighted, the floor heaped, the mantel loaded—I suppose there never was such a Christmas!"

"Cassie, you wouldn't taste this? It is the most delicious milk-toast I ever tasted in my life!" Tim said.

"If it tastes good to you, dearest."

"I don't know how Molly makes it. Molly, do you suppose you would show Sigma how you do it?"

"I think so, Tim." The women exchanged level quick glances of perfect comprehension, and there was heaven in their eyes.

"There isn't any more downstairs?"

"I don't know that I would now, Timmy," dictatorial and imperious Doctor Madison said mildly. "You can have more when I get back from the hospital, say at about one. Now you have to sleep—lots, all the time, for days! I'm going to take all the children to my house for dinner and over night. You're not to hear a sound. Look at the bowl, Cassie!"

She triumphantly inverted it. It was clean.

"Do you remember," Mary Madison asked, holding her brother's hands again, "do you remember years ago, when you used to eat my crusts for me, Timmy?"

"And is this bread upon the water, Molly?" he asked, infinitely satisfied to lie smiling at the two women who loved him. "I ate your crusts, and now you come and turn other crusts into milk-toast for me!"

"But don't you remember?"

He faintly shook his head. It was long ago forgotten, the little-boy kindness and loyalty, in the days of warts and freckles, cinnamon sticks and skate-keys, tears that were smeared into dirty faces, long incomprehensibly boring days in chalk- and ink-scented schoolrooms, long blissful vacation forenoons dreaming under bridges, idling in the sweet dimness of old barns. There had been a little passionate Molly, alternately satisfactory and naughty, tearing aprons and planning Indian encampments, generous with cookies and taffies, exacting and jealous, marvelous, maddening, and always to be protected and admired. But she was a dim, hazy long-ago memory, merged now into the handsome, brilliant woman whose fine hand held his.

"He used to fill his little pockets with them, Cassie. I can remember passing them to him, under the table."

"Our Tommy is like that," Cassie nodded.

"Think of your remembering—" Tim murmured contentedly.

He did not, but then it did not matter. It was Christmas morning, the restless dark night was over. Sun was shining outdoors on the new snow. His adored boys were happy, and the baby was asleep, and Cassie, instead of showing the long strain and anxiety, looked absolutely blooming as she smiled at him. Best of all, here was Molly, back in his life again, and talking of teaching the boys swimming, down at beloved old Beachaways. He had always thought, when he was a little boy, that no felicity in heaven or earth equaled a supper on the shore at Beachaways. The grown-ups of those days must have been hard, indeed, thought Tim mildly, drifting off to sleep, for he could remember begging for the joy of taking sandwiches down there, and being coldly and unreasonably—he could see now—refused. Well, it would be different with his kids. They could be pirates, smugglers, beachcombers, whale fishers, anything they pleased. They could build driftwood fires and cook potatoes and toast bread—

"Crusts, hey," he said drowsily. "Bread upon the waters."

"Bread is oddly symbolical anyway, isn't it, Molly?" Cassie said, in her quiet, restful voice. "Bread upon the waters, and the breaking of bread, and giving the children stones when they ask for bread! Even the solemnest words of all—'Do this in commemoration'—are of bread."

"Perhaps there is something we don't understand about it," Molly answered very softly. "The real sacrament of love."

She thought of the little crusts still in the pocket of the roll-top sweater, she looked at the empty bowl, and she held Tim's thin hand warmly, steadily.

"Christmas bread," she said, as if to herself.

Kathleen Norris
(1880–1966)

Kathleen Norris was born in San Francisco. During the first half of the twentieth century, she was one of the most prolific and popular writers of short stories and fiction in America. Among her books are *Mother* (1911), *The Sea Gull* (1927), *My San Francisco* (1932), and *Morning Light* (1950).

Lawrence J. Seyler
as told to Sue Philipp

THE NIGHT OF
THE BLIZZARD

The snow apparently had no intention of stopping—
so there went the midnight service on Christmas Eve.
Or did it? There were others unable to go home at
all—what about them?

*O*n the day before Christmas 1966 it snowed. And it kept snowing. All afternoon the blizzard whirled past my office window at Trinity Episcopal Church in Guelph Mills, Pennsylvania. I had already shoveled snow twice that morning so that the piling drifts wouldn't jam the church doors. It seemed a futile effort, though. Winds blew the snow in ever higher piles, and the road plows could not keep up with the storm.

The phone had been ringing all day with Christmas greetings, and already people were expressing their doubts about getting to church for our candlelight service: "Larry, the roads in our area may not be passable tonight. I'm afraid to risk them. Who knows, though—maybe it will slack off."

But it didn't. As the winter evening closed in, a nagging disappointment followed me around the empty church.

I knew I'd have to think about canceling the services. Once more I stared out at the storm. *Look at that, even a trolley is stalled. Everything's at a standstill.*

It had been a while since I'd heard a snowplow pass, and across the road a one-car trolley of the P & W line stood stranded. I could just barely make out its shape. If those P & W trolleys couldn't get through, what would happen to all the commuters coming home from jobs and last-minute shopping in Philadelphia?

My thoughts turned back to the evening service. In a world gone tinsel-crazy at this time of year, I looked forward to that one hour late at night, when men, women, and children came together to remember the birth of Jesus. That was the heart of Christmas, celebrated in a church full of people listening to the Nativity story, kneeling in prayer, and singing together "Joy to the World" and other old-time carols.

Yet how often Jesus got lost in the frantic baking and gift-giving, the parties and the shopwindow glitter that filled the holidays.

The phone rang. It was my wife, Cathy, calling from the rectory.

"Hi," I said. "How's it going over there?"

"The turkey is in the oven—finally," she announced, "and the kids are making cookies." She paused, then whispered, "When are you going to assemble David's fire truck?"

"Oh, after the service tonight," I told her.

"Larry, there must be three feet of snow out there, and the weather forecast is reporting more. How do you expect people to get through all of that!"

"This is what Christmas is about," I replied impatiently, "not turkeys and trucks! I'm going to have that service. Even if just God and I attend."

"Larry, the kids and I will be there, too."

"Thanks," I said, softening.

"Come on over in a few minutes for some coffee and cookies," she invited.

Tramping back to my office from the warmth of the rectory kitchen, I glanced over to the P & W track. "Good grief, that train hasn't moved!" I noted. Stomping snow off my boots, I walked into my office as the phone rang.

"Hi, Larry." It was Ed, our organist. "There's just no way I can get there tonight." He sounded as letdown as I felt.

"That's okay, Ed. Everyone else is snowed in too."

"Too bad," he replied.

"Yeah," I agreed. "You and your family have a good Christmas."

Good Christmas! Where was the good in this Christmas?

Going outside to push some more snow away from the front door, I saw the light from the stranded trolley. Were there people on board? Still?

I waded through drifts up to my thighs and squinted against the wind-driven snow. Peering through a window of the trolley, I pushed on the door to find about forty commuters huddled in clusters, deciding what to do. They were just on the verge of leaving the trolley to find refuge nearby; but, most of all, they wanted desperately to get home.

"Most of my kids' gifts are crammed in these bags!"

"My wife has planned the family dinner tonight. She's going to be upset."

"I haven't even begun my family's dinner. I wonder what they're eating."

"I was supposed to pick up my daughter. I hope she got home okay."

"I have a feeling we're going to be stuck here all night."

A teenager tried to doze.

I broke in: "Hey, listen everyone, I'm from the church across the street. Come on over and get warm!"

Relief spread over the passengers' faces as they gathered their belongings and piled out of the trolley, then waded and stomped a path to the church's door.

We got the coffee going down in the recreation

room under the sanctuary and as our guests began thawing out, I phoned Cathy.

"When that turkey is done, Honey, we could use it over at the church. We've got forty hungry passengers from the P & W and it looks like they'll be here through the night. They can't possibly get home in this storm."

"What? Sure, they can have the turkey. We'll bring the Christmas cookies, too. I'll call the neighbors. See you in a few minutes."

Then passengers began calling home, and I realized what a gap this storm had left in their holiday. Christmas plans had fizzled and I knew there was frustration felt at both ends of those conversations:

"Honey, I know we've never missed a Christmas together. . . . I wish I could be there with you and the kids."

"Hi, Dear. Everybody get home safe? . . . Yes, I'm okay. . . . You're decorating the tree? Yeah, I know, it's not the same without you, either."

". . . I know. I've got the kids' gifts. We'll just have to wait. . . . No, there's no way any of us can leave here. I miss you all so much. . . . We're in a church. They're taking good care of us here. . . . Now, don't you worry."

"Baby, don't cry. Daddy will be home just as soon as he can. . . . Be sweet. Give Mommy a hug."

One after another, they called to share a few moments with their families, to let them know they were safe. They wanted to be home, but it was obvious they would be spending the night. Travel was unthinkable. Nothing moved outside but the wind and the snow.

A few of our nearest neighbors fought their way over. Back and forth they came, bringing casseroles and salads, some of their own Christmas fixings, along with towels and toothpaste and orange juice and homemade breakfast rolls for the morning.

A neighbor confided: "We'd given up on getting out tonight. Even for the Christmas Eve service. We just assumed it would be canceled. But when we heard about these poor people trapped in the storm, well, we couldn't let them go without."

As people relaxed and as food was passed, spirits warmed, and gradually laughter filled the recreation hall. A party mood began sweeping through the group. One man came back from calling his wife to tell me:

"She doesn't believe I'm actually in a church. She hears all the laughing and thinks I'm at a party! Come on, Larry, and talk to her. You know what she said? 'You're lying! You haven't been in a church in forty years!'"

And then, before I knew it, it was time for the service. I'd almost forgotten it in the hectic scramble of caring for these people. They were in clusters of conversation. A few had stretched out on the six-foot mats used by children attending our church school.

I cleared my throat and interrupted: "There will be a Christmas Eve service in a few minutes. All of you are welcome to come."

The room became silent. People exchanged glances. In the midst of this hesitation, I left for the sanctuary to prepare for the service.

They all looked so comfortable. Would anyone come?

As I stood in the pulpit and turned the pages of the Bible to the Christmas story, Cathy and the kids came and sat on the front row. Then our next-door neighbors, Vivian and George Whittam, and their son, George, Jr., followed. Vivian sat at the organ and prepared to play. George turned on the tree lights, and their son lit the white candles surrounded by greenery.

A sparse group. Well, time to begin.

Then the door burst open and the trolley passengers came streaming in, smiling and whispering. And suddenly the church seemed almost full. Full of strangers, all brought by the snow to celebrate the birth of Jesus. And what a moving, worshipful time together! I will never forget it.

At 4:00 A.M. Christmas morning, after all of our guests were tucked in with mats and blankets, I finally got around to assembling David's fire truck. As I sat by the tree putting it together, I thought about the strange turn life can take, how some people had been kept away by the storm while others had been driven in by it.

And I thought about some of the remarks after the service. Like the woman who said if she'd managed to make it home, there would have been the family and the food and the gifts, but not Christ. To her, Christmas now meant something more than it had before the storm.

And to think that I had worried about the number of people who would be there to hear the Good News of His birth. I'll never worry again. For Christmas will always happen; it will not be denied. Christmas is greater than any storm—in nature, or in life.

Sue Philipp

Sue Philipp wrote for family and Christian magazines during the second half of the twentieth century.

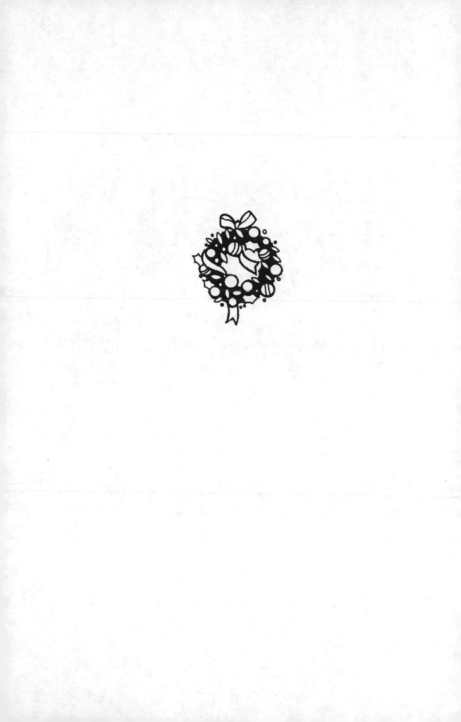

Florence Morse Kingsley

THE STORY OF
THE FIELD OF ANGELS

---

*Jerusalem and the great temple lay in rubble, but
children played as children have always played,
undisturbed by what may have happened in the past
as long as the present is pleasant.*

*Watching them was an old man who talked to
himself.*

*I*n the deep valley below Bethlehem an undulating meadow stretches east and west, its grass starred thick with blossoms in the days after the autumn rains. The villagers call it the Field of Angels, though to some it is known as the Place of the Star. In the days of the Caesars the turrets of Migdol Edar, the shepherds' watch tower, still looked down upon the place, though shepherds had long ceased to watch their flocks there by night.

Six miles to the north, behind the scarred shoulders of the ravaged hills, lay shamed and desolate Jerusalem. There was no longer a temple therein whither the tribes of Israel could go up to praise and magnify the name of Jehovah. Of all that great and glorious Zion there remained only a place for wailing by a ruined wall.

But flowers bloomed again in the red tracks of the Roman armies, and again there were little children to whom the horrors of that time of death were only as a tale that is told between waking and sleeping. When the sun shines in unclouded heavens, and myriads of flowers wave in the sweet wind, and the lark floods his acres of sky with heart-overflowing melody, what young thing will lament ruined temples or yet vanished cities, be they ever so glorious? And so, the children were plucking the first flowers in the Field of Angels with shouts and laughter.

In the dwarfed shadow of Migdol Edar sat an old man who talked with himself in the midst of his great silver beard, his blue eyes shining like twinkling pools amid the frosty sedge of a winter's morning. "The young things crop the blossoms like lambs," he muttered, and stretched his withered hand to gather a tuft of the white,

starlike flowers. Then he smiled to see a troop of little
ones running toward him, fearless as the lambs to which
he had likened them.

First came a tall girl of ten, her clear olive cheek
shaded by a tangle of curls; she held a flower-crowned
baby in each hand. Behind her lagged three or four
smaller girls and half a score of boys, shyer and more
suspicious than their sisters.

"Good sir, wilt thou gather flowers in the Angel
Field?" demanded the tall girl, fixing bright, questioning
eyes upon the stranger.

"Thou hast said truth, maiden," answered the old
man. "I have come from over seas to gather them. And
I will also tell thee one thing. Seest thou how many
blossoms grow in this low valley? There grows a shining
thought for every flower; these also would I gather."

The girl shook her head. "We have found no shining
thoughts in this field, honorable stranger," she said.
"Here are star flowers, and blue lilies of Israel, and
anemones purple and scarlet. There are no flowers like
those in the Angel Field. But I would that we might see
the shining things which thou hast gathered."

"Sit ye down upon the grass, every child of you," cried
the old man, his blue eyes beaming with delight, "and I
will show you my shining thoughts, for in truth they are
fairer than the flowers which perish in the plucking. See,
child, the blue lilies of Israel how they droop and wither,
and the star flowers drop their petals like early snow; but I
will show you that which can never perish. Look you,
children, I was no taller than yon little lad—he with the
scarlet tunic; and I wandered with the shepherds in this
field—which in those days was known only as the valley

of flocks—gathering flowers and minding the paschal lambs. They strayed not far from their mothers. Great Jerusalem was in its latter glory, and a marvelous bright star shone in the heavens. Wise men there were who declared that the star heralded the birth of Israel's deliverer, He who should be King of kings and Lord even of the Romans. The shepherds talked of these things in the night watches, and I, folded in my father's abba, listened between dreams.

"'Twas in this very spot we gathered on the night of which I will tell you. My father, the head shepherd, and very learned in the Psalms and Prophets, sat silent while the others talked softly of the flocks and of the weather, which was uncommon mild for the time of year, and of the pilgrims who had gathered out of all the provinces to pay tribute to the heathen emperor. The heavens were dark save for the great star which shamed all the rest into twinkling sparks. The young moon hung low in the west. I saw all this from the shelter of my father's cloak, and was content even as the lambs which lay close to the warm hearts of their mothers in the soft, damp grass.

"Suddenly my father lifted up his great voice. 'The Lord is in His holy temple: let all the earth keep silent before Him!' So spake he, and the others, marveling, held their peace. My young eyes were just closing in a dream of peace, but they opened wide at the sound of my father's solemn voice: 'Behold, I will send My messenger, and he shall prepare the way before Me: and the Lord, whom ye seek, shall suddenly come to His temple. Behold, He shall come, saith the Lord of hosts!'

"Then did the earth swoon and tremble—or so it seemed to my young fancy—and the light of the star on a sudden blazed forth with myriads of sparkling rays, of all colors splendid and rare, and radiance presently took shape to itself and became the figure of a man clad in dazzling garments who stood over against the sleeping flocks. He spoke, and his voice was as the voice of Jordan when he rolleth his spring floods to the sea. Every man of the shepherds was fallen to the ground with fright; but I lay unafraid in the shelter of my father's cloak and saw and heard all.

"'Fear not,' said the shining one, 'for behold, I bring you good tidings of great joy, which shall be to all people. For unto you is born this day, in the city of David, a Saviour, which is Christ the Lord. And this shall be a sign unto you: You shall find the Babe wrapped in swaddling clothes, lying in a manger.'

"Then were the heavens and the silent valley and the heights of Bethlehem filled with shining ones, who lifted up their voices in songs the like of which never yet fell on mortal ears. 'Glory to God in the highest, and on earth peace, good will toward men!' The anthem rose and fell in glorious waves of melody toward the star blazing in mid-heaven. The voices passed singing into the silence, and the shining forms, blent once more with the celestial rays of the star, wavered for an instant before our dazzled eyes, and were gone.

"My father was the first to recover himself from that trance of wonderment. 'Let us now go even to Bethlehem,' he said, 'and see this thing which is come to pass, which the Lord hath made known to us.'

"The shepherds girt themselves to depart, and I, creeping from the warm folds of the abba into the chill night, followed hard after them. Being low of stature—

for I was no higher than yon little lad—I saw a thing which the others perceived not: the soft, damp grass was starred with snowy blossoms both far and near where the feet of the angels had trod. I lagged behind to gather of them a great handful.

"The dim light of the inn swung half-way up the rocky steep, and there we waited in the darkness, my young heart beating loud in my ears, whilst my father parleyed with the keeper of the gate. There was no babe within, the porter said, and would have shut the door fast in our faces but that my father, being a man of authority and insisting that it was even as he had said, presently pushed by him into the khan. And indeed there was no babe in all the place, only pilgrims lying close to the sleeping-lofts and their beasts which crowded the courtyards.

"I pulled my father's sleeve and whispered to him that the angel said we should find the Babe lying in a manger. And in truth, my children, when presently we were come to the place where the great oxen were housed from the winter's cold, we found the young mother and the Babe wrapped in swaddling clothes lying in a manger. He, the Salvation of Israel—the Messiah—the Desire of Nations! These eyes gazed upon Him in His beauty. These hands touched Him as He lay asleep in the manger nestled in His soft garments on the yellow straw."

The tremulous voice faltered—ceased. The old man bent forward smiling, as if once again he gazed upon the world's Savior asleep in His manger cradle.

One of the girls laid a timid finger on the border of the pilgrim's cloak. "And was He—like other babies?" she asked in a low voice.

"Like other babies?" smiled the old man. "Yea,

verily, little one, He was fashioned in all points even as we are—thanks be unto Jehovah! Yet was He unlike— so wondrous fair, so heavenly beautiful was that Babe of Bethlehem as He lay even as an angel asleep in that humblest bed of all the earth. The milk-white blossoms I had gathered shone faint in the half darkness like tiny stars. I laid them at His feet and their fragrance filled all the place as incense."

The aged shepherd looked down at the flowers in his withered hands, his slow tears falling upon them like holy dew. Also he murmured strange words to which the children listened with wonder, albeit they understood them not at all. "Behold He was in the world, and the world was made by Him, and the World knew Him not. For by Him were all things created that are in Heaven, and that are on earth, visible and invisible, whether they be thrones, or dominions, or principalities, or powers. These things saith the Amen, the faithful and true witness."

Then the children stole quietly away one by one, till presently they were again at play amid the myriad blossoms of the star flower. But the old man rested beneath the shepherds' tower, while the shadows lengthened across the Field of Angels.

Florence Morse Kingsley
(1859–1937)

Florence Morse Kingsley of Medina, Ohio, was a prolific writer of short stories and novels. Among her books are *Titus* (1894), *Balm in Gilead* (1907), and *Neighbors* (1917).

Edith Barnard Delano

THE GIFT OF THE MANGER

Christine was weeping. She told her husband that they must go somewhere—anywhere—away from this house that held such tragic memories. Celebrating Christmas here would be an absolute impossibility. What could he do but tell her to pack her things?

This old story is set in the very early years of the 1900s.

*C*hristine's frail body bent slightly forward to meet the force of the gale. She kept her face lowered, shielded by her muff; yet now and again she raised it for an instant to glance upward at Norwood, with a bright flash of the eyes and a gleam of teeth. Invariably he met the look and warmed to it as to a flame, smiled back, or shook his head. To speak in the face of such a gale was all but impossible, yet once or twice she bent close enough to call out in her sweet, high tones, "I love it! I adore it!"

It was at such times that he shook his head. He was keen enough for adventure, good sport enough to meet it halfway, to make the utmost of it when it came; but this—the snow, the early fall of night, the upward climb over roads tantalizingly but half remembered—this was more than he had counted upon, and, truly, more than he wanted. He was beginning to wonder whether, even for Christine's sake, the journey was a wise one.

They had planned, weeks earlier, to take the noon train as far as River Junction, where his father, with the pair of sturdy gray horses, was to meet them for the eight-mile drive to the old home farm over the hills. But young doctors cannot always keep their best-laid plans, and Christine had waited in vain at the station while Norwood officiated at an entrance into the world and an exit therefrom—the individuals most concerned in both instances taking their own time. Christine, waiting beside the suit-cases, boxes, and parcels, whose number and variety of shapes unmistakably proclaimed Christmas gifts, had watched the express pull out of the station. Then, with a dull pounding at her temples and a barely controlled choking in her throat, she had gath-

ered up the Christmas impedimenta and gone home.
Norwood found her there an hour later, still dressed as
for the journey, and sobbing wildly in a heap at the foot
of the bed—his Christine, to whose courage during the
past ten months his very soul had done homage many a
time.

"I cannot bear it! I cannot bear it!" she had sobbed
out at last, when the tenderness of his arms had begun
to soothe her outburst of grief. "To be with your father
and mother, to make Christmas for the poor old
darlings, to work and keep busy all day—that was bad
enough; but I could have done that—"

"I know, dear, I know," he said, holding her firmly,
his professional sense alive to every pulse in the racked
body.

"But to stay here, where Teddy was last year—I
cannot, I cannot!"

"Christine!" he besought her.

"Oh, Ned, I have seen him watch me tie up every
parcel—I have heard him on the stairs—I have caught
myself wondering which toys he would wish for this
Christmas—and he isn't here! I cannot bear it! I cannot
stay here without him! I want my boy, my little boy—
my baby! It is Christmas eve—and I want my boy!"

And this was his Christine who, during the ten
months since the child had died, had faced the world
and her husband with her head held high, with a smile
on her lips and courage in the clasp of her hand! Not
once before today had he heard her cry out in grief or
rebellion—his Christine!

"Then we will not stay here," he said. "We will go to
the farm whether we have missed the train or not! We

will go to the end of the world, or beyond it, if that will help!"

"Ned! What do you mean?" she cried, drawing back from his clasp to look up into his face.

"It is only a matter of sixty miles or so, and it isn't yet two o'clock; we can make it with the big car!"

She sprang to her feet with a choking laugh, her hands on her throat, her eyes shining like stars of hope.

"Hurry!" she cried; and in scarcely half an hour they were on their way, the multitude of the Christmas bundles tumbled, helter-skelter, into the tonneau, she fur-clad and glowing beside him.

The big "sixty"[3] stood up to its task, and the first part of the journey was as nothing. It had been one of those winters when autumn prolongs itself into December, when people begin to talk of a green Christmas, and the youngsters feel almost hopeless about sleds and skates; but today, Christmas eve, the children's hopes had revived; a sudden drop in temperature, a leaden sky, an unwonted briskness among the sparrows—it might not be a green Christmas, after all.

That was one of the little things that Christine talked about along the way; and when the first few flakes of snow came wavering down she held out her muff, as if trying to catch them all, and laughed.

"Oh, see, Ned! We'll snowball each other tomorrow!"

But he had replied, "Let's hope that we shall have to postpone the snow-balling until we get to the farm, anyway. I declare! I had forgotten how steep these roads were!"

[3]Refers to horsepower

"Don't you remember them?" she asked. "Have you forgotten your way?"

He got the teasing note in her tone. "That's all right," he said, "but it has been many years since I came this way; and roadsides have a way of changing, even in Vermont; and with this storm coming along worse every minute, I am not anxious to negotiate them by dark."

"'Fraidy-cat," she laughed, and then cried: "Oh, see! The snow is coming! It's coming, coming, coming!"

It had come, indeed, on the wings of a quick, wild gust; its particles cut like bits of ice, and presently flew in swirling eddies beside the car and in front of it, and, for all their speed, built itself into little drifts wherever a curve or crevice or corner made a possible lodging-place. The snow pierced their barrier of windshield and curtains, and heaped itself on their fur wrappings, until swept away again by a new fierce breath of the storm. Then it was that Christine's cheeks flamed, but she bent forward to meet the force of the wind, and now and again turned to call out to Norwood that she loved it.

Night fell almost with the swiftness of a stage curtain, blotting out the distant hills, the pastures, the fields, and scattered houses; blotting out at last even the roadsides, its blackness emphasized by the ever-swirling, steadily descending snow. Once or twice Norwood stopped the car and got out to reconnoiter. Christine felt his uneasiness by means of that sixth sense of wifehood; yet all the while, by another of wifehood's endowments, she rested secure, serene in the feeling that all was well and must continue well with her man at the wheel. While side by side with his own feeling of uneasiness, Norwood was proud of his wife's courageous serenity, unaware in his masculine simplicity that her courage had its fount of being in himself.

Nobly the big car responded to their demand upon it, yet they had gone not more than a few miles beyond the last recognized sign-post when it began to show symptoms of reluctance, of distress. Norwood muttered under his breath, and once more Christine turned a laughing face toward him.

"It's a real adventure," she cried. "I do believe you are lost!"

Norwood's answering laugh held no merriment. "You're not so bad at guessing," he remarked, dryly. "Suppose you try to guess the way!"

Her keen eyes were peering forward through the veil of snow. "Here we come! I think I see a house ahead of us," she said. "We can ask our way of the people who live there."

"They won't know," said Norwood, with a man's pessimism. "Probably foreigners. Half the old places around here are bought up by people who can't speak English and don't know anything when they can."

"Oh, you just don't want to ask questions," said Christine. "Men always hate to! I never can see why!"

The day had held many things for him; now his nerves were beginning to jump. "All right, we'll ask," he said, shortly.

The car, in its inanimate way, seemed glad enough to stop. "I will run in and ask," said Christine, and Norwood was already busy over some of the mysterious attentions men love to bestow upon their engines.

"All right," he said, without raising his head.

But in a moment she was back. "It isn't a house, Ned! It's only a barn!"

Still bent over his engine, he replied: "House probably across the road. They often fix them that way up here."

But in another moment or two she was calling to him, above the voice of the gale: "Ned! Ned! There has been a fire! It must have been quite lately, for the snow melts as it falls on the place where the house was! How horrible to think of those poor people, burned out just before Christmas."

At that he stood up. "Burned out, is it? They may be camping in the barn. We'll see if we can't rout them out."

He went back a step or two and reached over to his horn, sending forth one honking, raucous blast after another. "That ought to fetch them," he said.

There was, indeed, an answering sound from the barn—trampling of hoofs, the suffering call of an unmilked cow. Christine went toward the denser blackness, which was the door.

"Hoo-hoo!" she cried. "Is anyone here?"

She held a little pocket flashlight in her hand, and threw its light here and there through the interior darkness. Norwood, still busy with his engine, was not aware when she went within; he was busy with mind and fingers. But all at once he sprang into a fuller activity— the activity of the man who hears the one cry that would recall him from another world; his wife had called to him, had cried aloud a wordless message which held wonder and fear, bewilderment, and—a note of joy?

He ran around the car into the open doorway of the

barn. The air of the vast space within was redolent with the scent of stored hay, the warm, sweet breath of beasts, the ghost of past summers, the promised satisfaction of many a meal-time. He could hear the movement of the animals in the stalls; the roof of the barn arched far above in cavelike darkness; in a quick flash of memory there came to him the story of another cave where patient beasts were stabled; and this was Christmas eve. . . .

Far back in the gloom there shone a tiny light. He was curiously breathless. "Christine!" he called, a quick, foolish fear clutching at his heart. "Christine!"

She answered with another wordless call that was partly an exclamation of wonder, partly a crooning. Blundering forward, he could see the dim outline of a form—Christine's form—kneeling in the dimness that was sparsely lighted by the pocket-light which she had dropped on the floor beside her. It was scarcely more than the space of a breath before he was at her side, yet in that space there had arisen another cry—a cry which he, the doctor, had also heard many times before. He felt as though he were living in a dream—but a dream as old as time.

"Ned, it's a baby! Look! Here, alone, in the manger!"

It was, truly, a manger beside which she knelt, and she held gathered closely in her arms a child which was now crying lustily. Norwood spoke, she answered, and together they bent over the little form. It had been warmly wrapped in an old quilt; it was dressed in a queer little dress of brilliant pink, with strange, dark woolen underthings the like of which Christine had never seen before. Its cradle had been warm and safe, for all the gale outside, and it had slept there peacefully in

the manger until the honking horn and this strange
woman had brought it back to a world of very cruel
hunger.

Norwood laughed aloud as its little waving, seeking
fists closed on one of his fingers. "Good healthy young-
ster," he said; "three or four months old, I should say."
Then he added, "Hey, old man, where are your folks?"

At that Christine held the baby more closely to her
breast. "Oh, I suppose it does belong to someone," she
said. "But, oh, Ned, I found it! Here in the manger—
like that Christ-child! It seemed to me that I found
something I had lost, something of my own!"

Norwood felt the danger of this sort of talk, as he
mentally termed it, and hastened to interrupt. "Sure you
found it!" he said. "That's just what the baby is trying to
tell you, among other things. He cries as if he were
starved. Can't you keep him quiet? My! How he yells!"

But Christine had sprung to her feet with the baby
still held closely to her in all its strange wrappings. She
was staring into the blackness of the barn. There must
have been a new sound, for Norwood also turned
quickly.

"Who's there?" he called. He had taken Christine's
light from the floor and now flashed it toward the
sound.

"All right! I will make the light," a voice called; and
with the careless noisiness of one who feels himself at
home, the newcomer stumbled toward a shelf near the
door and presently succeeded in lighting a dingy lantern.
It revealed him to be, as Norwood had foreseen, a
person distinctly un-American; and as they drew nearer,
his features disclosed themselves, though undoubtedly

old, as of that finished adherence to type which is the result, perhaps, of the many-centuries-old Latin ideal of human perfection—the type as distinct and clear-cut as a Neapolitan cameo.

"Well," said Norwood, jocularly, "quite a fire here, I see!"

The Italian raised shoulders and palms, alike disclaiming all responsibility and at the same time imploring the blessings of a benign Providence. "Oh, the fire, the fire! It burn it all up; it burn up everything!"

By gesture and broken words he made the story plain. "This morn' Maria send me to the River. I take the horse; I go. When I come back, I see the smoke way up. I whip the horse. The smoke! It flames up, up. I come to the hill. I see Maria run out of the house with the baby in her arms. She take the baby to the barn and she run back to Stefano. Stefano is in bed for three months—he cannot move. I whip the horse some more. I get to the house and jump down. I run to help with Stefano. *Ma! Dio mio!*" Again the gesture imploring Heaven. "The house, the floor, they come down. Maria, Stefano—all come down, all gone!"

He had made it graphic enough. They could see the quick tragedy of it, the wild rush of the mother taking her baby to its cradled safety in the manger, her dash back to the bedridden husband, the flames, the quickly charred timbers of the old house, the crashing fall. . . .

Christine could feel the blood rush back to her heart; her forehead, her lips, were as cold as if an icy hand had been laid upon them; she trembled, and strained the baby to herself as if it could still the sympathetic pain at her heart. Norwood, seeing her distress, moved closer, drew her into the curve of his arm; her head bent to his shoulder, and he could feel her silently crying. Before the revelation of the pitiful tragedy they were momentarily speechless; then Norwood began to question the man.

"But the neighbors? Why did no one come to help?"

The sidewise bend of the man's head, the opening fingers of his gesture, spoke as plainly as his words. "The others live far away—over the mountain. They cannot see the fire."

"That's likely enough, in these hills!" Norwood exclaimed. "But the barn? Why didn't the barn burn, too?"

"The wind takes the fire away from the barn—that way." He made an expressive gesture, pointing away from the barn.

"That's plain enough," said Norwood. "Well, I am mighty sorry for you, my friend. What can we do to help you? What are you going to do with the baby?"

The old man seemed to become aware for the first time of the child in Christine's arms. "Where did you find him?" he asked.

"My wife found him, back there in the manger where the poor mother laid him for safety, I suppose. What are you going to do with him?"

"He's not *my* baby!"

"My goodness, Sir! He is some relation to you, isn't he? Your grandchild, perhaps?"

"*Ma!* No! Maria, Stefano, they come from Ascoli! I"—he tapped his breast in a magnificent gesture—"I am *Siciliano!*"

Christine looked up and gave a little eager cry. "You

are not related? He isn't your baby, then, and you don't want him?"

"Wait, dear! Make sure, first, before you set your hopes too high." Norwood understood what was passing in her mind, and he added to the old man: "You are not related? What are you doing here, then?"

Again the shrug. "Stefano cannot work; he's very sick! I come, and Maria, Stefano, they tell me, 'Please stay to help. When Stefano is better, you can go!' So I stay—three weeks, maybe!"

Norwood thought quickly in silence for a moment; then he asked the man. "Do you know where Squire Norwood lives?"

The man nodded vigorously: "In a big house, a white house; over there—two or three miles."

"Can you show us the way?"

"Si!"

"Then come on! We will give you a lift and a place to sleep in."

Norwood led his wife and the child, now sleeping, as many centuries before another had led a woman and a sleeping babe. The beauty and wonder and mystery of it was not changed, not lessened because he led them through the snow on a modern dispeller of distance, instead of through burning wastes on a patient beast. She had taken the child from a manger on this Christmas eve; and it seemed a very gift of God.

The distance to Squire Norwood's house was only a matter of a few miles; yet it must have been an hour later when the two old people stood framed in the lamp-lighted door, hurriedly opened in response to the call of the car's horn.

"What's this? What's this?" his father's hearty voice called out. "Thought ye were coming by train, and Mother just broke down and cried when I come back without ye."

Bareheaded, showing the snow to be no whiter than his hair, he stepped out toward the big, dark shape of the car, which loomed enormous through the falling snow. Then he turned to stare after the shape which moved so swiftly past him and up to the shelter of the old wife's arms. Doubtless there were hurried words, questions, answers; but the fact of the mere existence of the baby seemed to be enough for the two women— one so lately new to grief, the other so nearly beyond it for all time. They stopped, then passed within; the lighted doorway was empty.

"I swan! Where'd ye get that baby?" the old man asked of his son.

Norwood explained; his father was quick with self-reproach that such a tragedy had transpired so near, while he, the friendly "Squire" of the countryside, should have been all unaware of it.

"Summertime I might have driven home that way. Mother and me often stopped to see how Stefano was coming along. But winters we always use the state road. It's longer, but better going. Sho! Mother will feel dreadful bad. She got to be real fond of Maria, what with the baby coming, and after. Maria used to tell as how they hadn't any folks, poor young things!"

"Are you sure of that?" asked Norwood, sharply. "Could not Christine—could we have the baby?"

His father's eyes held a sharp question, then became

quickly misty. "I *am* sure; but as selectman I can make it sure for ye beyond question."

The men's hands clasped; the squire coughed, and Norwood's doctor-sense was aroused.

"Why, Father, you are standing here without your hat! You go right in, and I'll put the car in the barn. I guess we can give this man shelter over Christmas, can't we?"

It was, perhaps, some three hours later, after his mother had worn out all her persuasion in trying to coax them to eat to four times their capacity; and after they had exhausted every detail of talk about the fire and the tragedy; and after they had disposed the be-ribboned parcels to be opened in the morning; and after Norwood had lifted his mother fairly off the floor in his good-night "bear hug"—it was after all of this that Norwood followed Christine up to the big south room, with its white-hung four-poster, and found her kneeling over the old mahogany cradle which had been his own. The old clock in the hall below struck twelve.

Christine arose, and laid her cheek against her husband's arm. "It's Christmas," she said.

And the baby, sleeping, smiled.

Edith Barnard Delano
(?–1946)

Edith Barnard Delano of Washington, D.C., wrote for popular and inspirational magazines during the first half of the twentieth century. Among her books are *Zebedee V* (1912) and *The Way of All the Earth* (1925).

SOMEWHERE I'LL FIND YOU

It was wartime, and the young soldier searched frantically all over San Francisco for his lovely fiancée. It had been a bad phone connection, so the words had been garbled. In only seventy-two hours he'd be shipped overseas. How could he possibly find her?

San Francisco! On a sunny day, it glowed like a gem beside the sea.

But at night, all was blacked out. For it was 1942. And the city—along with the nation—was at war.

Jim stared at the swirling waters coming in under the Golden Gate Bridge. At six-foot-four, with dark curly hair and dark eyes, he cut a handsome figure in his neat Army uniform.

Jim was billeted at the Presidio—for now. But two days after Christmas, he was scheduled to be shipped out to the Pacific Theater. Still, that was four days away. In the meantime, Carol was coming!

Carol, his fiancée! A slender beauty with blue eyes and golden hair the color of glowing Kansas wheat. They had met at St. John's College in Winfield, Kansas. He had grown up in an orphanage there. But a kind Trinity Lutheran Church member had paid his tuition to go to college at St. John's.

Then came the war. With Jim's enlistment in the Army and Carol's completion of her two-year college course, their paths were to separate. They had fallen deeply in love, though, and had become engaged on graduation night. Jim had given her a ring that night over dinner.

After that it was Fort Riley for him and a defense-plant job at Boeing in Wichita for Carol.

She had not been able to get time off until a few days ago. Next came the long train ride west. She was to arrive at 10 A.M. in San Francisco on December 24th—tomorrow. Jim had tried everything to get off duty so he could meet her. But the Army would not give him a pass until noon of that day.

So they had agreed on the phone to meet at the Cliff House. Yes, that was it. So romantic of Carol to choose this site. They had read about it—an historic restaurant overlooking the Pacific Ocean. Huge waves crashing on the rocks below. Barking seals sunning themselves on craggy rocks jutting out of the foam. Vessels in the shipping lane—and at times even whales—visible not far offshore.

The Cliff House! The afternoon of Christmas Eve! At least that's what Jim *thought* she'd said. The phone connection had been awful. Static. Dead air. Then static again. But she had shouted it to Jim: *"Cliff—! Cliff—!"*

Jim reached for his Eisenhower-type jacket and headed for a bus to take him to Fishermen's Wharf. He had a few hours free today. But not tomorrow morning—at least not until noon! "This is the Army, Mr. Jones!"

So Jim immersed himself in the sights and sounds of the city to offset his frustration.

He smelled the steaming crab pots and salivated over a shrimp cup on the sidewalk at Fishermen's Grotto #9. "I like Fisherman's Dwarf!" he heard a little girl tell her mother.

He took a cable car up the hills. Behind him he could see the cold, forbidding island of Alcatraz. He stared down Lombard, "the crookedest street in the world." And he walked up and down Market Street. Flower vendors hawked their wares. Paunchy Santas rang their little hand bells on each street corner, pointing to the tripod holding a red pot.

He paused at the huge Emporium windows. Piped-in music played carols. A child tugged on his mother's arm. "Look, Mom! There's an *activity* scene just like we have at church!"

Then he heard a crusty dowager remark, "What do you know about *that!* Even the *church* is trying to horn in on Christmastime!"

Near the window a placard read: "What is Christmas? Christmas is . . . wide-eyed children, fairyland magic, age-old music, and goodwill in the hearts of men."

"Is that *all* there is?" Jim mused. He moved away from the window. On the corner, he heard a man interviewing two young girls. "This is your radio man on the street!" he quipped. "Talking to the *people!* And what is the meaning of Christmas?" Giggling, one girl responded, "I don't know. Isn't that the day that Jesus died?"

Groaning, Jim moved on. There was some truth in the girl's answer. "Forgive us our Christmases," he thought, recalling another confused little girl saying her prayers at the end of a hectic day just before Christmas.

Disenchanted, he headed back to the Presidio. And the comments he had heard on Market Street haunted him the next afternoon as he headed out on a bus to the Cliff House to meet Carol.

He could hardly wait! How different some of those people's understanding of Christmas was from his and Carol's.

Looking out the bus, Jim saw a star on a flag in a window. Carol would be putting up a service star in the window for him. Then he recalled a story the pastor had told at a service at Immanuel Lutheran Church in Wichita.

A little boy and his father were out walking and saw many stars in the windows of the homes they passed. The boy started counting them. "What do the stars mean, Daddy?" he asked. And the father explained the meaning of a service star.[4]

Then they came to a vacant lot where there were no homes, no windows, no place to hang a service star. In the distance was a stretch of sky dominated by the evening star.

"Oh, look!" said the boy. "There's a star in *God's* window! Is that because God also gave a Son?"

"Yes," said his father. "God gave. He gave His *only* Son."

That was the meaning of Christmas. A child born in a crib to die on a cross, *for us*.

Finally the bus reached the Cliff House. Jim bounded out of it and almost ran into the restaurant. He moved restlessly from one spot to another, trying to find Carol, but she was not there. And that's how he spent the whole afternoon—looking and waiting for Carol.

It was the longest afternoon of his life. Several times he tried to phone Carol's parents or friends in Wichita whom she might have called. But then he remembered that her parents would be on the highway to St. Louis for Christmas. And no one else knew where she was.

Where could she be? All alone in a strange city. And on Christmas Eve!

[4]Families during World War I and World War II frequently hung a "service star banner" in a front window in their home. A blue star on the banner indicated that the family had a serviceman fighting in the armed forces; a gold star signified that the serviceman had died.

Only seventy-two hours were left now, and he'd be shipping out. He would stand on the fantail of the troop ship and look at the Golden Gate Bridge receding in the distance. Other soldiers would stand there with him, in total silence. And many would feel—they would just *know*—that they would never come back home again.

Sometime after 7 P.M., Jim pushed some food around on a plate, but he couldn't eat.

Where could Carol be?

On Christmas Eve?

And then it struck him. Of course! She would be in church! But what church? Where?

Hastily, he thumbed through the phone book, asking a waitress about the locations of the churches. St. Paulus Lutheran Church, Eddy and Gough. That might be it! The biggest, oldest Lutheran church, and nearest downtown, the waitress said.

Jim called for a cab and raced for the church. It was now nearly 8 P.M. He bounded up the few steps in front of the church, fog swirling around him. He stepped inside. The pastor was just concluding his sermon. The church was packed. It was a carol service, and the chancel was shimmering with dozens of candles. A massive Christmas tree soared near the huge, gleaming altar.

The pastor concluded: "So let the Holy Spirit prepare your heart now, as you go to Bethlehem tonight, and may you there enfold your Savior in the manger of your faith. Amen."

The congregation rose and began singing, "It Came Upon the Midnight Clear."

Was Carol here? How could he find her among some six hundred people? He couldn't wander up and down the aisles and disturb people's worship. He looked up. The balcony! Of course! It was a huge, U-shaped, wrap-around sort of balcony, one that could afford him a look *back* at the faces of the people. He half-ran through the narthex and leaped up the creaking stairs to the balcony.

"That glorious song of old . . ." the congregation sang.

Jim edged along one of the walls of the long balcony and, arriving at the front, peered back at the faces in the crowd.

"From angels bending near the earth to touch their harps of gold . . ."

Jim could almost feel the brush of angels' wings. *For he saw Carol.* There she was. Third row, right on the center aisle. This time he bounded down the stairs and had to force himself to walk—not run—down the aisle.

Edging in beside her, he saw her gasp as tears welled up in her eyes.

"Jim!" was all she could say.

He hugged her fiercely. Could he kiss her? Here—in *church?* Well, on their wedding day they would kiss right in front of the altar.

Jim kissed Carol gently, tenderly, warmly. And he didn't let her go.

"Look up, for golden is the hour, come swiftly on the wing . . ."

Finally, they slowly pulled apart. Everyone around them was singing lustily, beaming with smiles and tears as they watched the tall, uniformed young man and his lovely betrothed.

"And all who take this gift will hear the song the angels sing."

The carol ended, everyone sat down, and the ushers began to receive the offering.

"Where *were* you this afternoon?" whispered Jim.

"At the hotel—like I said."

"Hotel! *What* hotel?"

"The *Clift* Hotel!"

"You said *Cliff House,* I thought."

"And I tried to reach you at the Presidio, but no one knew. . . ."

"That telephone connection," said Jim. "So *that's* it."

They both nodded, understanding now what had happened.

Ushers passed them, bringing the plates down the aisles to the altar. The pastor had a prayer, then pronounced the benediction.

Then a hush fell over the congregation. For the lights had been dimmed. Everyone's eyes were focused on the glowing altar and sparkling Christmas tree.

And high in the balcony a child's voice, soft and clear and calm like an angel's, started singing "Silent Night, Holy Night."

One by one, people in the congregation joined in the beautiful, age-old carol.

> *Sleep in heavenly peace,*
> *Sleep in heavenly peace.*

Jim squeezed Carol's hand.

And so it was a good Christmas Eve.

Not like other Christmas Eves back in Kansas.
But it was a good Christmas, after all.

Donald L. Deffner
Donald Deffner wrote for family and inspirational
magazines during the second half of the twentieth
century.

Joseph Leininger Wheeler

CHRISTMAS SABBATICAL

In ancient Judea, even the land was given time off every seven years—it was called a sabbatical. So how about humans: How long should they go without one?

*I*t was good to get away.

Away from lesson plans, advising, tests, essays, committees, term papers, and the tyranny of bells. It had been a long time coming, this sabbatical leave. It was scheduled to come every seven years, but for him seven years had come and gone once, twice, and now finally—and almost unbelievably—the third proved to be the proverbial "charm." He had off not only the summer but also the fall semester.

It had not been easy, for times were tough and the administration begrudged giving *anyone* time off. Even— make that *especially*—those teachers whose classes always filled first. Those old reliables VPs fondly labeled "cash cows."

Had it not been for this dual insurance, tenure and cash cowhood, Ryan would most likely never have pushed his luck by insisting on the sabbatical. Jobs had a way of disappearing when professors stayed away too long. Even if the Academic Policies Committee had to temporarily close a program, minor, or even major in order to do it. And it hadn't helped a bit that he was the current chair of the department.

May had been an incredibly hectic month. Not only did he have to get his grades in, he also had to orient the acting chair, get a consensus on who would teach what classes the following year, submit book orders for those classes, rough out his own lesson plans for spring semester, and tidy up his office (a temp would be using it while he was gone). Oh yes, and he had to promise the president's secretary that he'd keep her current on his whereabouts.

But now with all that finally done, he was free! Free

for the first time in twenty-one long years. He felt like trumpeting Martin Luther King Jr.'s ringing words: "Free at last! free at last! thank God almighty, we are free at last!"

Money was not much of a problem, for he'd been depositing money in his sabbatical account for many years. Besides that, from his grandfather's estate had come a modest legacy.

But no structure! So relentlessly regimented had the last twenty-one years been that he had long ago determined that when the sabbatical finally came, all structure would end.

So . . . what would he do with seven months?

TIMBERLINE LODGE
MOUNT HOOD, OREGON

Always, it seemed, he'd loved old hotels. This one was born in 1936, during the depths of the Great Depression. All across the country, weary men asked for jobs that did not exist. Finally, President Roosevelt established the WPA (Works Progress Administration), a vehicle for putting men to work and salvaging their self-respect. Building this 74,000-square-foot hotel at the 6,000 foot elevation of Mt. Hood was a way of employing hundreds—eventually a thousand. FDR himself came there to dedicate it on September 28, 1937. But it didn't open to the public until February of 1938.

On an early June evening, Ryan sat on a crimson sofa in front of one of Timberline Lodge's six fireplaces and looked up at the great chimney, ninety-two feet high. The snow lay six feet deep outside. Hard to believe that he'd left the Napa Valley, ninety-three degrees in the shade, only two days ago. How his new candy-apple red Oldsmobile Bravada had purred as it scampered down Howell Mountain and north toward Calistoga.

Warmed by the crackling fire, Ryan could feel the accumulated tension of the years beginning to ebb away. His truant mind drifted, not toward the future but toward the past—to another great hotel, the Ahwahnee of Yosemite (reminding one of the Shangri-la monastery of *Lost Horizon*), opened ten years before Timberline. He had stood next to one of the massive Great Lounge fireplaces that December twenty-five of twenty-six years before. Moving toward him, as dreamlike as though she walked across moonbeams, was a lovely blonde attired in Christmas red, snow beginning to melt from her sweater.

Suddenly he raised his hand and said, "Stop just where you are! I want to drink in the vision of what you are." She stopped, her deep blue eyes twinkling, and she looked at him as though he contained her world. Lines came to him, and he repeated them from memory:

> *She is coming, my own, my sweet;*
> *Were it ever so airy a tread,*
> *My heart would hear her and beat,*
> *Were it earth in an earthy bed;*
> *My dust would hear her and beat,*
> *Had I lain for a century dead,*
> *Would start and tremble under her feet,*
> *And blossom in purple and red.*

"Tennyson, isn't it?"

"Yes, from *Maud*."

And when he had taken her into his arms and kissed her, a lone tear of happiness had glistened on her cheek. . . . *Oh, how? . . . Oh, where? . . . Oh, when did I lose her?*

Now, more than a quarter of a century later, he was confronted, unaccountably, by that scene—no state-of-the-art movie screen could have brought it back with greater fidelity. The scene that now, unaccountably, returned to him once he freed his mind to roam where-soever it wished. *Why did I lose her, God?* he wondered. Was it because she had hardly ever seen him without a book in his hands? Was it because he had tackled both a master's and a Ph.D. during the five years of their marriage? She had worked so hard to pay for it all. And he hadn't been much company when she'd come home dead tired. Her *needs? Why should* she *have needs? Wasn't that what she signed up for—her Ph.T. (Putting Hubby Through)?*

Without so much as one empty frame between, his thoughts fast-forwarded five years to another Christmas. But this time the lens of memory saw things he'd never noticed before. He had just hauled in a tall white fir, and Perry Como was singing "I'll Be Home for Christmas" on the stereo. He had looked across at her through the tree branches they were decorating and . . . *I don't remember seeing that before!* Her face had looked thin, her shoulders drooped, and her eyes—her sad eyes—had lost their bubbling joy of life. It was only a moment, that glimpse, then she quickly lowered her eyes. Neither of them had said anything—how he wished they had! He had figured there would be plenty of time to talk about it after Christmas.

Three days later he'd come home from bowling with a colleague to a house that was ominously quiet. He'd called her name. No answer. He had continued calling, hurrying from room to room. "Allison! Allison!" he had called. Only silence. Finally he had entered their bedroom. Only one light was on, a bedside lamp. And beside it was an envelope bearing his name, and the handwriting—that beautiful cursive handwriting—was hers. Somehow he had known even before he opened it. Slowly, his blood freezing, he had opened the envelope, dreading what he would find. The letter was not long, and a tear had blurred several of the words, words that would sear their way into his memory:

> *Dear Ryan,*
>
> *It's over. You'll never know how hard I've tried to make it work. But you have drifted away from me. You treat me as though I am merely another piece of furniture. I am supposed to give, give, give while you take, take, take. You do not cherish me anymore. In fact, I seriously doubt that you even love me anymore.*
>
> *Time after time I've tried to discuss these things—not once did you listen to me. Instead, you either tuned me out or walked out of the room.*
>
> *You are not the man I thought I was marrying. You have a brilliant mind, but your heart has no room inside for anything but yourself. At any rate, had I known five years ago that you were incapable of loving anyone but yourself, never would I have entrusted my life into your keeping!*

How fortunate that we decided to wait until you finished your dissertation before having children. Well, now you have that wretched piece of parchment—that diploma that means far more to you than I ever have.

You are welcome to it. Cuddle up to it on cold nights. Tell it how much it is adored. May it be the comfort you never found in me.

I took some money out of the bank. Half our savings. We don't have much, as you well know. I took some of my clothes and the things I treasure most. And my beat-up old car. The rest is yours.

Don't ever try to contact me or find me again. You represent a closed chapter in my life.

Allison

He never had.

How empty that house felt without her! He didn't know until it was too late that she was the very soul of the house! Without her lovely, loving presence it was dead, dead, *dead!* He couldn't stand it. He gave notice and moved out several days later.

But life moved on, even though he felt that the bottom had fallen out of his world. Before, he had taken Allison for granted, but now that he had lost her forever, he would have sacrificed everything he owned—including his academic degrees—to get her back. For years he'd wake up in the middle of the night, reach for her, call her name, and realize once again how empty his life had become. The nights—oh, the nights—were always the worst.

In time, however, since he disregarded her words and

attempted to expunge her summation of himself, he steeled himself against her memory. In justifying his own actions, he automatically condemned hers. Love coalesced into icy cold anger, anger into malice, and malice into sulphurous hate—hate that even his closest friends didn't know he harbored inside, hate that he was subconsciously ashamed of himself.

Now he mused, *C. S. Lewis was right in* Till We Have Faces: *We* all *wear masks—even in front of ourselves.*

For a time after this unwelcome self-revelation, mists closed in on his past.

Not long after she left, he'd landed a teaching position—and that had become his life.

"Coffee, sir?" A waiter intruded on his memory. With a jolt, as though he had just time-traveled back from the past, awareness of the present flooded back in on him. Blankly, he nodded. "With cream and sugar, please."

Dinner followed. Afterward, he returned to his room. So sleepy was he that he didn't even make it through the ten o'clock news.

DRIFTWOOD SHORES
ON THE OREGON COAST

In years past, every time he drove north out of Napa Valley, almost invariably he would veer westward toward Florence, Oregon, and check in at Driftwood Shores. This trip proved no exception, only this time he reached it driving west from Portland, then south on Coastal Highway 101.

Driftwood Shores was fogged in and drizzly. He decided to stay inside. Outside the dining room he could see those brave souls who refused to be defeated by the elements. Attired in heavy sweaters or coats, they made their barefoot way down the long beach until the mists closed in behind them. In the distance, a foghorn's mournful sound could be faintly heard.

Later on, in his room, he opened the deck doors so he could listen to the breakers. A big storm was blowing in.

I don't care, let 'er come. The bigger the better! Maybe it will keep my past from tormenting me tonight.

He got his wish. The wind howled and screeched, the rain viciously slashed the windows. So loud were the breakers that it sometimes seemed they were thundering into his third-story room. Having always loved storms, he merely threw another blanket on and burrowed in. But he slept very little. Nothing felt right with his soul; each oncoming wave seemed to attack the flimsy foundation posts he'd built his life upon.

Next morning, the only evidence of the night's tempest was the mass of driftwood, seaweed, kelp, and shells on the beach. About midmorning the sun broke through the fog. Soon after breakfast, he headed down the beach. How good the sand felt under his bare feet. Seagulls and sandpipers swirled around him, sometimes flying north and waiting for him, and sometimes flying south. Hours passed before he found a sand dune to his liking. There he settled down, out of the wind. Having been battered by the night, he leaned back against the warm dune with a tired sigh, and before he knew it, he was asleep.

The shadows were long before awareness returned, and he woke slowly, by degrees. Then he ate the lunch prepared for him by the Driftwood Shores chef. How good it tasted!

He pulled a notebook and pen out of his knapsack and fingered a fresh sheet of paper. That paper represented over six and a half months of his future. What should he do with them?

Travel. It had always been in his blood, but he never seemed to get very far away. Now he had no time constraints and plenty of money—he was free to roam wherever whim should take him. He pulled out a map of the world and unfolded it.

Hmm. Mustn't forget my promise to myself: no schedule! But at least I can study this map and pick out some places I've always wanted to see. Let's see. . . . His eyes lingered on places like the Canadian Rockies, Glacier National Park, Yellowstone, the Grand Tetons, and Colorado—and, farther east, the Gulf coast, the Mississippi River, the Smokies, and New England. It would be his first time there. Then across to Europe. London first, then the Continent. Bavaria at the height of the fall colors. *Then,* he told himself, *I'll play it by ear till Christmas.*

He decided to hit the road again the next day.

CHÂTEAU LAKE LOUISE
ALBERTA, CANADA

How impossible to find any place more beautiful than this! Photographs just don't do it justice!

He'd risen early in order to photograph the sunrise as it first burnished the peaks with volcanic fire, then flowed down like slow lava to the glacier-fed emerald lake far below. He felt alive as he had not in years. And tinglingly aware of the fragility of life and the increasing pace of time (every year passing more quickly than the one before). Sort of like those old playground merry-go-rounds he used to play on as a boy. All the kids would get on, and an adult would begin pulling it faster and faster, so fast that everything would blur, his stomach would feel queasy, and he'd just let go, flying into space, then whumping into something, or someone, tumbling over and over. He wondered if life was like that: if, after a while, one just gave up and let go? Perhaps it was because of failure to accomplish much of any value. Hadn't he, more and more, periodically looked back and admitted to himself, *I just can't see much of value there. Again, I just went through the motions. But having neither wife nor children, I'm accountable to no one but myself . . . and my employer. So who's to care if I just whirl and whirl until I finally let go, whumping whatever's in the way?*

For some inexplicable reason, on this golden morning he found that he *did* care. He rummaged around in his knapsack for something that had caught his eye in the hotel gift shop the evening before. *Ah, here it is!* It was a beautifully illustrated placard of a poem he'd first read during his college years but had never paid much atten-tion to before yesterday. *Don't really know what possessed me to buy it, but in the stillness of this breathtaking dawn, perhaps it will speak to me. All I know about it is that it was written by India's greatest poet, Kalidasa, and that people usually refer to it as "The Salutation to the Dawn."*

Finding a rock jutting out into the lake (still smooth as glass, unruffled by even the ghost of a breeze), he sat down and slowly read the poem, determined this time to discover its meaning and why it defied all the odds by still being alive after a millennium and a half.

Look to this day!
For it is life, the very life of life.
In its brief course
Lie all the verities and realities of your existence:
The bliss of growth
The glory of action
The splendor of beauty.
For yesterday is but a dream
And tomorrow is only a vision,
But today well lived
Makes every yesterday a dream of happiness
And every tomorrow a vision of hope.
Look well, therefore, to this day!
Such is the salutation to the dawn.

After finishing it, he again looked out across the lake, seeing but not seeing. Then he read the poem another time, more slowly, seeking to dissect its meaning.

How true! Every day a miniature lifetime—with a beginning (like this crystalline moment), a middle, and an end. Still he wasn't satisfied. He read it again, even more slowly, his brow wrinkled, as he attempted to grab the poem by the scruff of its neck and shake the truth out of it. Finally, his forehead smoothed out: *I've got it! Kalidasa is convinced that dwelling in the past is an incredible waste of time, for absolutely nothing can be done about it! Take me, for instance. How much energy I've siphoned from my todays in order to dwell in my yesterdays! Let's see, how did Kalidasa put it . . . 'Yesterday is but a dream.' True, it may be a dream one may return to, but it is not a dream that can be changed. That, I've got to think about for a bit. Wonder if one could ever change a dream that appears frozen for all time in the past. Nah . . . impossible!*

By now, he was like a pathologist searching a body scan for a clue. *Next Kalidasa turns to the future and declares that tomorrow is only a vision. Kalidasa is deep! Just as is true with our dreams of yesterday, our visions of tomorrow are ephemeral and devoid of substance. So living in our tomorrows is just as much a waste of time as living in our yesterdays, for we are powerless to act in either place!*

Ryan stopped, jolted by a sudden realization that he had squandered most of his life. Not in terms of acquiring knowledge, but in his priorities—learning how to live.

Now that Kalidasa had disposed of both tendencies, living in the past and living in the future, Ryan was forced to confront the present, something he had always avoided. But Kalidasa had made a solemn promise: Living each moment to the fullest spread of its canvas makes "every yesterday a dream of happiness and every tomorrow a vision of hope."

"In other words," Ryan concluded out loud, "today 'well lived' is the answer. But that sounds almost too good to be true! . . . But isn't that just what that poem—the one I wrote in my journal years ago—is all about? That God can get us through each today—if we just ask Him?"

Once more he rummaged around in his knapsack. For years now, he'd been practicing what he preached to his students: he carried his journal with him everywhere he went. At the back, he wrote down poems, sayings, epigrams, and figures of speech that caught his attention. After some time, thumbing through those well-worn pages, he found it:

I was regretting the past
And fearing the future.
Suddenly my Lord was speaking:
"My name is I AM."
He paused. I waited.
He continued,
"When you live in the past
With its mistakes and regrets,
It is hard. I am not there.
My name is not I WAS.

"When you live in the future,
With its problems and fears,
It is hard. I am not there.
My name is not I WILL BE.

"When you live in this moment,
It is not hard. I am here.
My name is I AM."

Helen Mallicoat[5]

After reading it, Ryan just sat there, unable to take on even one additional thought. Numb.

❄ ❄ ❄

It was some time before awareness returned. He rose to his feet, one of which had apparently gone to sleep on a rock. It took quite a bit of stamping to awaken it. In need of action instead of further contemplation, he decided to hike around the lake and up to the Japanese teahouse high above it.

[5]Used by permission of author

It was midafternoon before he puffed his way to the summit where the teahouse awaited him. Along the way, scores of squirrels scurried out to greet him, then stood up on their hind feet and begged for peanuts. Fortunately, he'd been forewarned. Even so, the peanuts ran out before the squirrels did. Once the sun dipped below the mountain, cold began to seep in. It was time to descend. Each turn of the downward path brought a new vista. Some were almost breathtaking. Far across the lake was that jewel of a hotel, for generations called The Château Lake Louise. Certainly it looked like a French château. It was almost dark before he reached it.

Next morning, he checked out and headed south toward Mount Rainier.

MOUNT RAINIER PARADISE INN
WASHINGTON

The road to the venerable hotel (first opened to the public in 1917) had only been open for a matter of weeks. So much snow gets dumped on Paradise Valley that the inn has to be closed and boarded up each winter. The hotel was almost lost during the 1960s when the National Park Service proposed demolishing it. A storm of rage all across the Northwest put a quick stop to that, and it was restored instead.

Out a great window Ryan could see majestic 14,411-foot Mount Rainier, towering above the hotel. The mountain, home to the greatest single-peak glacier system in the United States, is so mighty that it creates its own weather.

Several days had passed since leaving Lake Louise. In

that interim he had given his mind a recess: *Gotta give all these heavy thoughts time to sift through my subconscious.*

But now it was time to pick up where he had left off. He reflected, *How glib I've been in classes when I've discussed epiphanies—those rare moments of insight that rock a life with all the potency of a Richter eight earthquake. Those moments you later look at and say, 'What an experience that was! You know, if that day had never been, how different my life would be!' But now it's happened to me.*

So what do I do about it? Do I just pretend the epiphany never happened? Or do I find a crossroads and switch to another track?

❋ ❋ ❋

For the first time in twenty-one long years, he took off the self-justifying glasses he had worn so long and looked back to that long-ago letter from Allison without anger, vindictiveness, self-justification, or hate. And for the first time he stared at the person he had been with honest eyes—admitting to himself that Allison had been right and he wrong. Everything she had written was true then—and, worst of all, was still true now. At least until now.

The strangest feeling came over him. It seemed he could actually feel twenty-one years of acid begin to drain out of his body. Over the years that resentment, anger against Allison and unwillingness to forgive her, had turned into the deadliest kind of venom. Over time it had gradually poisoned, in one way or another, every act and thought of his life. Now for the first time, these inner knots loosened and he began to tremble. The trickle of escaping acid became a flood. Some time later, when the flow finally ebbed, he felt clean both inside and out.

Forgiveness came next. *He forgave Allison.* Completely. Forgiving himself proved to be much harder, and brought home the need to seek out Allison and ask for forgiveness. *Funny—for all these years it was she I was unable to forgive. Now the shoe is on the other foot! I must track her down, wherever she may be after all these years.* Years ago, he had heard she was remarrying, so the trail to her might be difficult. But he knew he must find her, for real peace would not come to him until he pled for her forgiveness.

But merely knowing that he *should* do something was not enough. It never had been. Procrastination had always defeated his best intentions, so why should this time be any different? . . . But come to think of it, there *was* something that might make this time different!

Several months earlier during a lecture, Ryan had come face-to-face with a legendary thought-leader who had been a contemporary of Christ's: the Rabbi Hillel. Hillel had left for posterity what has become known as "The Eight Magic Words." He now searched for them in his journal. *Oh, here they are! Two questions the speaker guaranteed would change my life—if I internalized them, repeated them over and over all day, for thirty days. Then I could forget about them, for they'd thereafter be an integral part of who I am and how I act. Two simple questions. Seems almost impossible that eight little words could change my life, but if they've lasted two thousand years there must be something in them that transcends time.*

If not me, whom?
If not now, when?

The speaker pointed out that we are confronted each day with hundreds of choices. These choices add up to who we are and what we become. Each time we have the opportunity to grow, to be of service, to make a difference, but fail to do so, we shrink in stature. Each time we accept such a challenge, we increase in stature. It is that simple.

The speaker told us that the second question must invariably follow on the heels of the first. If I don't do it now, when will I? That's a no-brainer. Given my well-documented procrastination record, if I don't do it now, I'll never do it at all! Learned that sad truth about myself years ago. Furthermore, when am I ever likely to find time to do it if I fail to do it now?

That brought Ryan to the crossroads he had been pondering. Without question, if he was ever to turn his life around, it would have to begin with Allison. If he didn't seek her out and ask her forgiveness for his treatment of her, certainly no one else would ever do it for him. In a nutshell, Hillel's first question placed the entire responsibility for rectifying the wrong on his shoulders. Hillel's second question left him no wiggle room whatsoever. The inner peace he longed for could come at no lesser price.

❄ ❄ ❄

Two days later, he was back at Paradise Inn. He had gone to Seattle, where he had retained the services of a reputable detective service. Before leaving its office, he had filled out an extensive questionnaire. He'd been

assured that they would do their best to track down
Allison. When they found her, they'd let him know via
e-mail. He'd left his cell phone at home—for good
reasons. Laughingly, he had quipped, "A cell phone and
serenity are oxymorons."

He found himself welcoming each day as a gift from
God, a one-of-a-kind gift that would never be dupli-
cated. And there was no guarantee that there would
ever be another for him. A poem by an anonymous
author perhaps summed it up best:

> *The clock of life is wound but once.*
> *And no one has the power*
> *To tell just when the hand will stop*
> *On what day—or what hour.*
> *Now is the only time you have.*
> *So live it with a will.*
> *Don't wait until tomorrow.*
> *The hands may then be still.*

After having blocked Allison out of his thoughts for
so many years, he found it strange how the draining of
his inner acid had opened the door to memories of her.
The good times returned in the interstices of his days
and nights. Her laugh, so joyful and infectious. The
delicious bread she made. Her obsession with sweaters,
and the scarlet one she loved most. Her shyness with
people she didn't know. Her green thumb—*especially*
with geraniums, which she kept alive all year long. Her
thoughtfulness—never forgetting a birthday, anniver-
sary, or special day; never forgetting to express gratitude.
Her faith in God, the very rock of her existence. Her

intense love of family. Her constant yearning for affection: At any hour of the day or night, she'd come to him and say, in that adorable way she had, "Ryan, I'm hungry for you." (He realized now that he had repulsed her and her great need of being loved so often that she had quit telling him of her hunger.) Her innate neatness. Her love of old bookstores and antiques. The way she sang when she was happy—come to think of it, she hadn't sung much during that last year. The way she cried at sad books, movies, and music. The contrast between her homing instincts and her love of wandering. Her determination to grow, to learn new things each day of her life. The faraway look he sometimes caught on her face when she felt alone. The tremble of her dear lips when she was near tears. How quicksilverish she was—never the same twice; how rapidly her moods would change. The way she'd cling to him during thunderstorms. Her love of all God's creatures, *especially* kittens and puppies; "Kitty" had been his pet name for her, for how she had loved to snuggle and how she had purred when happy (ruefully, he now realized that she had purred very little that last year). He remembered the way she had looked at him (when she thought he didn't see), as though he were everything she had ever wanted. The endearing way she had had of insisting he have his arm around her before he read out loud to her. Her dreamlike contours. The hair he had loved to kiss—always with the fragrance of springtime.

Not all at once, but singly or in clusters, these pent-up memories streamed back. They warmed his heart. But it was a bittersweet warming, for they represented a past that could never be again. It was as though he had once been as rich as King Midas but had not known it until his riches grew wings and he was left destitute.

THE STANLEY HOTEL
ESTES PARK, COLORADO

How incredibly blue is the sky of Colorado's high country! Outside the great dining-room window was a snow-capped vista that could never grow old. Never in a hundred years! He'd just returned from Trail Ridge Road overlooking Never Summer Range, the top of the world. The Rockies, he feared, were in his blood to stay.

In the foyer of the hotel was a deep green Stanley Steamer, looking like it had just come off the showroom floor (if indeed there were auto showrooms some ninety years ago). The Steamer deserved to grace the lobby of the grand old hotel it had helped build.

Now Ryan sat in the grand wood-paneled lobby of the Stanley. Complementing the dazzling white hotel, the lovely town of Estes Park looked like a little bit of transplanted Switzerland. He stepped into one of its shops for a double-decker ice-cream cone—rocky road and cookie dough. As he sat on a bench outside savoring it, the thought suddenly came to him: *How Allison would love this!* She had such a weakness for ice cream. In fact, her father had once quipped, "Allison has never met an ice-cream cone she didn't like." And it was as though a cloud dimmed the ultramarine sky.

Only moments later, as he walked along the singing creek that eternally romances the town, he almost said it out loud: *How Allison would love this!* Her dream house, she had always maintained, would be on a mountaintop, with a creek running by so she could go to sleep listening to it, and with the sea far below. Invariably he'd retort, "You and your impossible dream!"

Strangely enough, no longer did it seem like he was alone on this sabbatical, for Allison was always turning up in the most unexpected places and times. Nights especially, for whenever a full moon graced the sky, she had always wanted to be loved, basking in its luminous glow all the while. That night an almost full moon lit up the sky outside his hotel window. Her absence was such a torment that he was not able to sleep until almost dawn.

It was during that seemingly interminable night that the realization came to him: *Now that it's too late . . . I know I've never stopped loving her. . . . It's the real reason why I've never remarried. No one else could possibly take her place! So why, dear Lord, am I such a slow learner? "Block-head" would be a more apt term. Why has it taken me almost twenty-one years to discover this?*

A poem that his preacher father had read to Allison and Ryan at their wedding in Yosemite came back to him. His father had taken Allison to his heart as the daughter he'd never had. How brokenhearted his father and mother had been when they heard the news of their divorce. And Ryan had blamed Allison for it all. Now it was too late: His parents lay sleeping in a coastal California cemetery.

But the poem he could still recite by heart:

> *Woman was made from the rib of man.*
> *She was not created from his head to top him,*
> *Nor from his feet to be stepped on.*
> *She was made from his side to be equal to him,*

> *From beneath his arm to be protected by him,*
> *Near his heart to be loved by him.*

Author unknown

And he had failed —utterly failed—to protect her, even to love her.

From the detective agency came news of dead end after dead end. No one appeared to know where Allison had gone after she'd left San Francisco. Or what name she might bear now.

BASS ROCKS OCEAN INN
GLOUCESTER, MASSACHUSETTS

Summer slipped to its close; thousands of miles had clicked away on the Bravada's odometer. Ryan found that the synthesis of Kalidasa, Hillel, and Mallicoat was revolutionizing his life; every moment glistened like a polished pearl—it was like moving from black-and-white television to technicolor. Yet he had gone from sea to shining sea, and still no trace had been found of Allison. It was as if she'd disappeared off the face of the earth.

Yet . . . she was still with him. Especially this night, with the waves crashing in upon the rocky Massachusetts shore. Earlier he had walked down the shore to the lighthouse, exulting in the sights, sounds, and smells of the sea. All along the way, Allison had walked beside him, her face alight with joy. He could not see her, true, but he *felt* her presence. How she loved the sea!

This somber mood that had come upon him—was

there anything in prose or poetry that could perfectly capture it? He opened his journal and found it on the third page from the back. It was one of the few truly memorable quotes he had found in Baroness Emma Orczy's *The Scarlet Pimpernel:*

> In some moods, the sea has a saddening effect upon the nerves. It is only when we are very happy that we can bear to gaze merrily upon the vast and limitless expanse of water, rolling on and on with such persistent irritating monotony, to the accompaniment of our thoughts, whether grave or gay. When they are gay, the waves echo their gaiety; but when they are sad, then every breaker, as it rolls, seems to bring additional sadness, and to speak to us of the hopelessness and pettiness of all our joys.

That night, he was lulled to sleep by the waves shattering their force on the unyielding rocky shore.

Early the next morning, he was awakened both by the sound of the waves and by the sunrise flooding into his room. He rose and went out to meet the new day—meet it with his newfound carpe-diem joy.

When he returned later from breakfast at Twin Lights, an e-mail message awaited him:

> *First lead we've found. In 1991, she moved to Kansas City. We found the apartment she lived in. A year later she left the area. No one appears to know where. We'll stay on the trail.*

CHÂTEAU FRONTENAC
QUEBEC CITY, QUEBEC, CANADA

Coming here was a dream come true. Ever since
boyhood he had fantasized about this dreamlike castle
far above the waters of the St. Lawrence River. High up
in one of the towers was his room, and there he could
dream: *How she would love this place, this history, this room,
this view!* He had showed her a picture of it once, and
she'd sighed, "If only we weren't so everlastingly poor
and could afford to go there. I'd ask for the highest
room they had. And you'd have to pry me away from
the window with a crowbar before I'd leave."

"Here's your window, dearest . . . but I forgot my
crowbar," he teased, then sheepishly turned away as he
realized that his dream world and the real world were
merging. Which was real and which was not, he no
longer seemed to know.

Later as he walked up and down the steep, windy
streets of the old city, he could almost feel her hand in
his and hear her delighted responses to all they saw.

Back in the great hotel, he saw children everywhere
he looked. Curious, he asked the concierge, "Surely
these children can't afford to stay here and pay these
rates!"

The concierge laughed and said, "No, monsieur, they
are our guests. We make it possible—charge them *nothing.*"

"Huh?"

"Well, it's this way," the man said, and a faraway
look came into his eyes. "Many years ago the owner of
this hotel had a vision of what might be, if only he had

the courage to do it and could persuade his associates to be willing to wait."

"Wait for what?"

"Patience, monsieur. Patience to wait until those children grew up."

"I don't understand."

"Oh, monsieur, they persuade their parents to bring them back. They marry here, spend their honeymoon here, return here on anniversaries, and bring their children—even grandchildren!—here. It paid off years ago." He stopped, looking fondly at one wide-eyed little girl looking up with awe in her face, and continued, "See her? She's our future."

THISTLE TOWER HOTEL
LONDON, ENGLAND

It was mid-September, and he'd crossed the Atlantic on the *Queen Elizabeth II*. He was beginning to wonder about himself: Several times onboard he'd had opportunities for romance. One woman, in particular, was breathtakingly beautiful. But something held him back. Allison held him back, for she was along. Just yesterday, leaning over the railing at the sight of England emerging out of the mists of the English Channel, words spoken during their courtship days came back to him: "Ryan, promise me that someday—if you *ever* go to England—you'll take me along!" To himself he mumbled, "You're getting to be a bit of a nuisance, Allison. How am I supposed to enjoy this sabbatical with you popping up all the time?" But he smiled so her feelings wouldn't be hurt.

Several days later, after having seen many of the sights

of London, he was back in his hotel room, staring out at the Tower Bridge outside his window. Night had fallen, and the bridge had lost its distinctiveness. It was like an impressionistic painting by Whistler.

He spoke into the night: "I just can't understand. Years ago, I was told that Allison had remarried. She's almost certainly still married. Why can't I get her out of my system? Long, long ago, it was all over. . . . *Leave me, Allison!*"

But Allison didn't leave. She remained by his side, looking at him reproachfully.

Next morning, there was another e-mail:

> *Good news. She moved to Mobile, Alabama, in June of 1994. She left in August of 1996. We don't yet know where she moved. For some reason, she was still using her maiden name.*

I don't understand it. Why would she be using her maiden name if she had remarried? Is she that modern?

Ryan spoke to the room: "It's time to hit the road. Can't wait to step into that Jaguar convertible promised by the car rental agent. We'll head for the Chunnel tomorrow! And Allison, don't pout: the right front seat is yours."

NEUSCHWANSTEIN CASTLE
BAVARIA, GERMANY

It was October, and Ryan had been reveling in the glorious autumn colors of the Bavarian Alps as he drove his silver Jaguar. Now Ryan was living in the fairy-tale world of King Ludwig's Neuschwanstein, the world's most famous and most imitated castle. Ryan had become acquainted with the castle's head curator onboard the *QE II*. Just before he had disembarked, an invitation had been slipped under his stateroom door: "I've invited a few people to be my guests at Neuschwanstein for a week, during the height of the fall colors. Would be pleased to have you join us." The dates were given, and he was asked to confirm by e-mail.

So here he was (pinching himself to see if all this was real), high up in a part of the castle tourists are never permitted to see. There was a sudden knock on the door. He opened it. One of the castle guides handed him a letter with a U.S. stamp and postmark. After thanking the guide, he closed the door, moved to a chair by the window, and studied the envelope. It was from the office of the president of his college! His heart sank. Was he in trouble? Was he being let go? Fearing the worst, he slowly opened the letter. Inside was a smaller envelope addressed to him in care of the president's secretary. It bore neither the name nor the address of the sender. Even more apprehensively, he opened this one. Then his hand froze in midair—it was from *her!*

He postponed reading it for several minutes. Why, he didn't really know. Perhaps because as long as he didn't read it, he could continue to live in the dreamworld with her. Because of the letter, she might leave him . . . a second time.

Finally, he read it anyhow, as slowly as possible.

> *Dear Ryan,*
> *For some time now I've had the strange feeling that I was being stalked. Several individuals I'd known some*

*years back contacted me and told me someone was trying
to track me down. The whole thing has given me more
than a few sleepless nights. Who could it be?*

*Early yesterday evening, as I walked into my apart-
ment, I heard the phone ringing. It was George at the
front desk. Skipping all preliminaries, he said in a whisper, "Listen carefully, Ms. Beaupre. You've told me to
be on the alert as you felt someone was stalking you.
Well, a certain such person is here in the lobby right now.
He asked me about you. Suspicious, I told him to talk to
the condo manager. He's waiting for the manager to call
him in. I called the manager on the sly and asked him to
delay, hoping I could alert you."*

*"I'll be right down!" I responded, and I was out the
door and down the hall to the elevator in milliseconds.*

*The long and the short of it is that I caught your
detective red-handed. The manager and I confronted him
together and got him to "'fess up." Otherwise, the
manager threatened to call the police and accuse him of
stalking and harassing. Obviously, he is a new detective
and is not yet slick enough to deal with such a confronta-
tion. He cracked. Gradually, we got the story out of him.
Then we let him go, but not before informing him that if
he revealed my whereabouts to his agency, a suit for inva-
sion of privacy would be filed by my attorney immediately!*

*I then called the college where you teach and rang the
president's secretary. A woman with a familiar voice
answered the phone. She'd roomed next door to me my
freshman year in college. After small talk, I asked her if
she'd do me a favor. She answered, "Of course!" I told
her you'd been trying to get ahold of me but didn't know*

how to get in touch with me. She told me you were on sabbatical. Assuming she had your schedule (or could get one), I asked if she'd be willing to forward my letter to you. If you've received this, she was successful.

Very briefly and to the point, What's up?

You may respond to my e-mail address.

HOTEL SPLENDIDO
PORTOFINO, ITALY

High above the shimmering, silver blue Gulf of Genoa on the Italian Riviera, looking out his hotel window late this November afternoon was Ryan, a pensive look on his face. Much had happened since Neuschwanstein.

He'd spent a *lot* of time on his first e-mail, for so much was riding on it. Then he'd waited hours, days, and weeks before her response came. Her next one didn't take as long. Lately, e-mails shuttled back and forth on a daily basis. Gradually, they opened up to each other. Eventually Ryan told her the entire story of his sabbatical: what he had been, how and why he had changed, and what he hoped to someday become. Her responses had been more guarded. That is, until her last one. It lay on the table before him. He didn't need to reread it, for he had almost memorized it.

Dear Ryan,

You have no idea how happy your latest e-mail has made me. Now—at last—I am emboldened enough to tell you the truth about me. Here are some details you may find interesting:

I'm a travel agent in Nag's Head—no cracks from

you, sir!—North Carolina. Knowing my love for travel, you shouldn't be surprised at my profession.

Finally, I'll answer your oft-repeated question: I just couldn't do it! Called off the wedding just thirty-six hours before it was to take place. Hated to do it to the groom, for he was wonderful to me. And I genuinely loved him. There was just one catch: I loved someone else even more. I've just never been able to stop loving you, hard as I tried. And I did try hard. For year after lonely year, I tried. And other men came into my life and tried to help me put away the memories of that long-ago sad life.

None of it worked. One reason has to do with my upbringing and my faith. I had sworn before God to devote the rest of my life to you and no other. For me— guess I'm different from so many of my friends—divorce failed to quiet my conscience. I still felt married to you.

Years passed. You still had not remarried. Oh yes, I kept track of you. I had my own (unpaid) detectives who kept me abreast of what was happening in your life. I prayed daily that God would bring resolution: either bring you back into my life or free me to find someone else. Neither happened.

It didn't help that the portrait of you painted by my correspondents was no different from the Ryan I had known at the time I left. Self-centered and unkind. Insensitive. Judgmental and hypercritical. Unforgiving. Unwilling to empathize. Almost devoid of tenderness. I just could not even consider going back to that! I would rather die lonely!

More years passed. I never even felt you were giving our memories a second thought. After all, twenty long years had passed! But I had my pride; I told my closest friends that under no condition should they let you know where I was—unless you became a different person. And I wasn't very hopeful about that, for only God could cause such a miracle to happen!

Some months ago, however, something strange began to happen: I kept getting the feeling that you were thinking about me—positively rather than negatively. As time passed, these vibes came more and more often. I just couldn't understand it. I prayed more and more, imploring God to explain, direct. On one memorable October night, early in October, I did a "Jacob": I wrestled with the Lord all night and told Him I just could not let Him go until He brought me peace. I think I wept more that night than I have anytime since those dark days before I left you.

Just before dawn, when I was almost too exhausted to stay on my knees any longer, the answer came—as clearly as though my dear Lord said it out loud in my bedroom:

My beloved child, your prayers are answered. Ryan loves you, but not as he did before. He is no longer the self-centered man you once knew. A miracle has occurred. Just wait, my very dear Allison. You won't have to wait much longer. My peace I leave with you.

And peace came to me. It surprised me not at all to find your detective in the lobby the very next day. But I was perverse enough to give you a rough time for the almost twenty-one years of loneliness and heartbreak you

*put me through! And I must admit I was somewhat lack-
ing in faith: even though God had assured me you had
changed, I still wasn't sure. So I came at you from all
directions, trying to find out if the new you was real—or
merely an act. Eventually I became convinced that God
had indeed worked a miracle in your life.*

Twilight stole in before he again became aware of his
room in the eagle's nest of the former Benedictine
monastery that Orient Express Hotels had purchased in
1983. As he looked down upon one of the most
enchanting towns in the world, he thought, *I must bring
her here! I must! How many years I have to make up for! But
I mustn't hurry this. A false or premature step could wreck
everything. I must court her all over again.*

THE AHWAHNEE HOTEL
YOSEMITE, CALIFORNIA

For weeks the e-mails had been flying back and forth.
And then, once Ryan was again on U.S. soil they began
exchanging phone calls and letters.

Now it was December 25, and a ruggedly handsome
man with dark hair beginning to fleck with gray stood
by a window table looking out at the falling snow.
Twenty-six years ago tonight he had married a radiant
Allison in this very hotel. His mind swept back through
the years to that more-precious-than-he-had-ever-
dreamed night when she had shyly entrusted her life
into his keeping.

Then, as now, snow had fallen all day. Then, as now,
the great hotel was decked out to greet the season of the
Christ child. But twenty-six years yawned between, and

twenty-one years had come and gone since she walked out of his life. *He* had certainly changed; he was half a century old! And she was forty-six.

But in only moments—unless she'd had second thoughts and changed her mind—there would come the moment of reckoning. He found himself assailed by wave after wave of sheer terror.

Oh, Lord! What if, when I see her, I recoil? I know I've gone way too far to ever turn back. I could not possibly break her heart a second time! Were she prematurely old, disfigured by a fire, or a quadriplegic, I'd love her still. But . . . uh . . . I represent a real work-in-progress, Lord—I've a long ways yet to go. Is it . . . is it too much to ask—that the years won't have been too hard on her? You know what I'm trying to say: Are all men like me?

In the doorway, some distance away, there was movement. A slim figure in Christmas red was moving slowly toward him. The candlelight was kind, softening the impact of the years. Lady Clairol was helping too: her hair was still golden. She was lovely still.

Suddenly, he raised his hand and said, "Stop just where you are! I want to drink in the vision of what you are." She stopped, her blue eyes twinkling. And once again she looked at him as though he contained her world. Lines came to him, and he spoke once again:

> *She is coming, my own, my sweet;*
> *Were it ever so airy a tread,*
> *My heart would hear her and beat,*
> *Were it earth in an earthy bed;*
> *My dust would hear her and beat,*
> *Had I lain for a century dead;*

> *Would start and tremble under her feet,*
> *And blossom in purple and red.*

Unable to resist the temptation, she said, somewhat roguishly, "Tennyson, isn't it?"

Neither did he resist. "Yes, from one of his least known works."

Caught off guard, eyes widening, she responded, "Oh?"

"Yes, it's called—" and he dropped down on one knee—*"Will You Marry Me?"*

❄ ❄ ❄

HOW THIS STORY CAME TO BE

I didn't use to tack on such a thing as this to my stories, but I've had such a good response to my 2001 anthology, *The Twelve Stories of Christmas* (where I did this for each of the first twelve Christmas stories I wrote myself), that I've decided to continue the tradition. If enough readers write in that they like it, chances are I'll continue it.

This particular story didn't come easy—none of mine do. In fact, during the last fourteen years, I've only written twenty-one (and those were almost all written because I had deadlines to meet).

For six months of 2002, I thought I had my 2003 story all but ready to write. As it turned out, it was ready to write but it was also too long—long enough for a full-length book. So I decided to keep it in escrow for that purpose.

So there I was in early October, still without even a

concept for the Christmas story. But I wasn't worried, for over the years of my writing partnership with God, never once has He let me down. One golden October morning, with the aspens aflame outside our mountain-top home, I prayed, *Lord, here I am again, asking for help on yet another story. You know full well that I refuse to write a story that doesn't come from You. Only Yours have the power to speak directly to the heart and motivate the reader to aspire to live in tune with Your will. So I turn this story over to You. I'll wait in stillness for You to give me the plot.*

I did. And slowly, it came. The male protagonist came especially easy, since teaching is my profession. The female protagonist was longer in coming into focus. Since I am a fifth-generation Californian on both sides of my family and I was born in the Napa Valley, the setting was a natural for me. But God did not see fit to give me the plot full bloom; rather, He revealed it to me gradually each day of the week it took to complete the first draft. Each day, I would ask for wisdom, and each day vision came for that segment, but no more. I came to the middle of the story and still had absolutely no idea how it would play out.

I've always loved old hotels and special places to stay. We have actually visited or stayed at all of those men-tioned in the story except for Paradise Inn and Hotel Splendido, but we'd *like* to stay at them as well. Due to an obvious oversight on the part of Neuschwanstein's staff, our visit there ended without their extending us an invitation to remain. The conversation with the Château Frontenac concierge about the children actually took place during our visit there.

I've had a few sabbaticals of my own, and thus I can

testify to the euphoria that results from getting one—
and to the epiphanies that often result from leaving the
academic squirrel-cage wheel for a time. I shall never
forget a two-hour discussion I had about seventeen years
ago with one of America's leading consultants (even
then, Fortune 500 CEOs were paying him two thousand dollars an hour). He told me that he could
condense all his wisdom into one directive to these
CEOs: "Get out of your squirrel cages and *go somewhere*—I don't care where!—but go! And each year,
travel for one week more than you did the year before.
And I *guarantee* that the insights gained by this act will
make your corporation more successful than it was the
year before!" I've never forgotten those two hours.
They now live again in this story.

I never cease to be amazed by God's incredible
choreography. His timetable rarely mirrors ours. I spent
thirty years researching a book, *Remote Controlled*, that
sold only eleven thousand or so copies. I poured into it
not only all that I had learned about the impact of television on the American psyche, but also all I knew
about time management—as well as my personal philos-
ophy of life. Some of those who have read it label it a
life-changer. If it is, it is because God cowrote it. But
from time to time I've wondered, *Lord, why did you have
me pour so many years into a book that so few people have
ever read?*

Well, I wasn't very far into this story before my Lord
spoke to me: *Weave into this story the very heart of*
Remote Controlled—*the three most powerful statements
you've found about time management and growth during your
lifetime. I want this to be more than just a Christmas story—I*

want it to be a life-changing story (our Remote Controlled *unfinished business).*

So I did. It is no hyperbole to say that each of the three sources—Kalidasa's "Salutation to the Dawn," Hillel's "The Eight Magic Words," and Mallicoat's "I Am" poem—came to me as an epiphany. If I have accomplished anything of note in my life, it is because I internalized each of them. And the shift away from what I was to what I became was every bit as abrupt as Ryan's.

A sidelight here is that over the years Helen Mallicoat of Wickenburg, Arizona, has become one of my most cherished friends. She has been amazed by her poem. Hallmark has printed it in the millions (both in card-size and poster-size), and hardly a day goes by that she doesn't hear of it bobbing up somewhere around the globe. She has never felt that the poem was hers—but rather, a gift from God.

Even though I'm not a certified counselor, many have come to me for counsel over the years—especially when I've traveled alone, such as during sabbaticals. And one thing I've seen again and again is this: Unwillingness to forgive (if continued long-term) will inevitably result in a person's body filling with a corrosive acid. Eventually it will destroy the one who harbors such an unforgiving spirit. In fact, in Scripture God warns us that if we fail to forgive, He, in turn, will find it impossible to forgive *us*. I felt impressed by God to incorporate this into the story as well.

And last, and anything but least, in spite of our media elite's continual efforts to get us to treat marriage as a mere throwaway, the vows meaning no more than an attorney's legalese, I have observed firsthand, over and over, the phenomenon of divorced individuals being haunted the rest of their lives by those vows directed to their former spouses, family, friends, and God. And they find it extremely difficult to buy into the contention that divorce papers invalidate those sacred vows. This, too, I felt impressed by God to weave into this story.

Thank you, Lord.

Most helpful in researching this story was Christine Barnes's insightful *Great Lodges of the West* (Bend, Ore.: W. W. West, Inc., 1997).

FOCUS ON THE FAMILY®
Welcome to the Family!

It began in 1977 with the vision
of Dr. James Dobson, a licensed psychologist
and author of best-selling books on marriage,
parenting, and family. Alarmed by the many
pressures threatening the American family,
he founded Focus on the Family, now an
international organization dedicated
to preserving family values through the
life-changing message of Jesus Christ.

•   •   •

For more information about the ministry,
or if we can be of help to your family, simply
write to Focus on the Family, Colorado
Springs, CO 80995 or call 1-800-A-FAMILY
(1-800-232-6459). Friends in Canada may write
Focus on the Family, P.O. Box 9800, Stn. Terminal,
Vancouver, B.C. V6B 4G3, or call 1-800-661-9800.
Visit our Web site at www.family.org
(in Canada, www. focusonthefamily.ca).

We'd love to hear from you!

Joe Wheeler fan? Like curling up with a good story? Try these other Joe Wheeler books that will give you that "warm all over" feeling.

HEART TO HEART STORIES OF LOVE

Remember old-fashioned romance? The hauntingly beautiful, gradual unfolding of the petals of love, leading up to the ultimate full flowering of marriage and a lifetime together? From the story of the young army lieutenant returning from World War II to meet his female pen pal at Grand Central Station in the hope that their friendship will develop into romance, to the tale of a young woman who finds love in the romantic history of her grandmother, this collection satisfies the longing for stories of genuine, beautiful, lasting love.

Heart to Heart Stories of Love will warm your heart with young love, rekindled flames, and promises kept.
0-8423-1833-X

HEART TO HEART STORIES OF FRIENDSHIP

A touching collection of timeless tales that will uplift your soul. For anyone who has ever experienced or longed for the true joy of friendship, these engaging stories are sure to inspire laughter, tears, and tender remembrances. Share them with a friend or loved one.
0-8423-0586-6

HEART TO HEART STORIES FOR DADS

This collection of classic tales is sure to tug at your heart and take up permanent residence in your memories. These stories about fathers, beloved teachers, mentors, pastors, and other father figures are suitable for reading aloud to the family or for enjoying alone for a cozy evening's entertainment.
0-8423-3634-6

HEART TO HEART STORIES FOR MOMS

This heartwarming collection includes stories about the selfless love of mothers, stepmothers, surrogate mothers, and mentors. Moms in all stages of life will cherish stories that parallel their own, those demonstrating the bond between child, mother, and grandmother. A collection to cherish for years to come.
0-8423-3603-6

HEART TO HEART STORIES FOR SISTERS

Heart to Heart Stories for Sisters is a touching collection of classic short stories that is sure to become a family favorite. These stories about sisters and the relationships that bind them together are perfect for reading aloud to the whole family, for giving to your own sister, or simply for enjoying alone.
0-8423-5378-X

HEART TO HEART STORIES FOR GRANDPARENTS

Grandparents and grandchildren share a special bond—because there's something almost magical about that relationship. From the story of a man who lovingly cares for his grandmother after she develops Alzheimer's disease, to the tale of a woman whose advice helps her great-granddaughter decide which man to marry, this beautiful volume will touch your heart and encourage you to savor the time you spend with family members—of all generations.
0-8423-5379-8

HEART TO HEART STORIES FOR TEACHERS

Good teachers open up the world for their students—and leave a permanent legacy in the hearts and minds of those whose lives they touch. This moving collection of stories portrays the inspiring relationships between teachers and their students, from the one-room schoolhouse to the college classroom. Perfect for reading alone or sharing with a favorite teacher.
0-8423-5412-3

CHRISTMAS IN MY HEART
Volume IX

From the tale of the orphan boy who loses a beloved puppy but finds a loving home for Christmas, to the narrative of an entire town that gives an impoverished family an unexpectedly joyful Christmas, these heartwarming stories will touch your soul with the true spirit of the season. Featured authors include O. Henry, Grace Livingston Hill, Margaret Sangster, Jr., and others.

Christmas is a time for families to take time to sit together, perhaps around a crackling blaze in the fireplace, and reminisce about Christmases of the past. Enjoy the classic stories found in this book and understand why thousands of families have made the Christmas in My Heart series part of their traditions.
0-8423-5189-2

CHRISTMAS IN MY HEART
Volume X

Christmas in My Heart, vol. 10 will bring a tear to your eye and warmth to your heart as you read the story of a lonely little girl who helps a heartbroken mother learn to love again, or the tale of a cynical old shopkeeper who discovers the true meaning of Christmas through the gift of a crippled man. Authors include Pearl S. Buck, Harry Kroll, Margaret Sangster, Jr., and others.
0-8423-5380-1

CHRISTMAS IN MY HEART
Volume XI

The Christmas season is a time for reflection and
peace, a time with family and friends. As you
read the story of a father desperately searching for
the perfect gift for his little girl, or the account
of two brothers who learn a meaningful lesson
about God's love from a pair of scrawny
Christmas trees, you'll expereience anew the
joys and meaning of the season.
0-8423-5626-6